When th
with hi

Jarting boldly stood up, the revolver hidden behind him, and called out. "Whoever you are, come out and let's talk. I know you're not one of those Utes. You're a white man. Come on. We can make a deal that will be good for both of us."

Other Day stood and stepped out from behind the rocks.

"Well, well, well. Logan. I never would have suspected it was you. What do you want? Why did you kill these men?"

"Because it's scurvy rabble like you who turn Indians into drunks and killers. Leave them alone, damn it."

"Why are you so interested? What have the Utes done for you?"

"I'm half Pawnee, and I hate white men who act like you. I hate Indians who let white men take advantage of them. I'm—"

Before Logan could finish the sentence, Jarting whipped his pistol out to blow the 'breed away. . . .

The *Breed* series by Ned Stone:

BREED
BREED #2: MOUNTAIN MASSACRE
BREED #3: BLOOD ON THE RAILS

BREED 4

ONE-MAN JURY

NED STONE

LEISURE BOOKS NEW YORK CITY

A LEISURE BOOK®

March 1991

Published by

Dorchester Publishing Co., Inc.
276 Fifth Avenue
New York, NY 10001

Printed in the United States of America.

CHAPTER ONE

Other Day Logan pulled back on the reins and the bay gelding slowed to a stop. The half-breed studied the small valley below him. On the distant side, a group of buildings stretched out along the only street of what appeared to be a town. A few houses clung at the ends of the string, trying to achieve a certain air of respectability for the community that had arisen on the pristine landscape. Railroad tracks—which entered the valley beyond the town, passed through the valley, and left on the 'breed's left-hand side—appeared to be the only reason for the town's existence. A few cattle pens and a station tried to balance the row of unpainted buildings. One two-storied building sat close to the depot, across the rails from the water tank.

Other Day knew he was coming to cattle

country, and more than likely to the south and west sides of the hills that ringed the valley, he'd find cattle spreads. Behind him, in the north, he'd passed through rugged country, foothills of the Rockies, and even farther north he'd left a railroad job and the woman who had looked so much like Belle Doolin, his dead sweetheart.

Logan shook his head. He hadn't thought of Belle for the last few days, and now that he had, he wondered if he'd ever get over the loss of the woman he'd loved. A growl rumbled deep in his chest and he shook his head, trying to dislodge the memory and send it back to the dark recesses of his mind.

Large white clouds sailed by overhead and Other Day looked at the sun. It would be down in a few hours. He might as well head for that reprobate town below and get a hot meal and maybe a bath. It'd been over two weeks since he had left the town of Hades and the railroad, and he hadn't cleaned up much since. After a shave, a hot bath, and a good meal, he'd be ready to head back out to the countryside for the night. He nudged the bay in its side and the horse stepped out once more.

When the half-breed approached the town, he noted the lack of activity along the only street. A few cow ponies were tied to hitching rails, their heads bowed in the late afternoon heat, but there weren't any people walking about. He didn't find that particularly surprising since he could see nothing that would make someone want to be out in the heat. It appeared there was only one saloon in business and that was where the horses were tied.

The 'breed walked his gelding down the length of the row of buildings. He wondered what the name of the town might be since he saw no signs of any sort on the building fronts. Off to his left where the railroad tracks lay, the station and other structures stood alone. When Logan neared the depot, he saw the name *Flea Hill* painted on a board hanging from the near side. Without stopping the bay, he turned in his saddle and looked over the buldings he'd ridden past. He didn't like the town, not at all. There was something upsetting to the 'breed about it. Not that he liked towns or groups of people. He preferred his own company to that of other men and women because they would invariably turn out to be two-faced and untrustworthy. Theron Cullen, the hunter who was murdered by the enemies of the railroad, had been an exception. Theron had had child-like qualities about him that Other Day had found to his liking. Children were the only humans Other Day Logan would trust to any degree. When he had found Theron hanging from a tree, whipped to within a breath of being dead, Other Day had sworn vengence and had won it when he beat Theron's murderer into a whimpering lump.

But there was something about Flea Hill that made the 'breed feel hopeless. That was it: there was an air of hopelessness about the town. Maybe he'd just stop for a shot or two of whiskey and a couple of beers and get the hell out of there. He rode past the station and water tank, which sat opposite the two-storied building, the railroad tracks separating them. It was a courthouse and jail combined. Well, Logan didn't want anything to do with the law. He'd keep his nose under his own hat and not worry about anybody's business. Trying to help others usually got him into trouble.

Angling the horse toward the livery, Other Day swung out of the saddle and walked into the barn. "Hello?" he called out.

A thin old man walked out, nodded, and said, "Howdy. Bed your horse down for the night, stranger?"

"I don't know about that yet. Give him a rub-down and brushing and some oats. I'll be back later."

The old man looked at him closely. "You a 'breed?"

Other Day turned and stared at him, said nothing, then spun on his heel to walk to the saloon. He hated white men for what they had done and were doing to the red man. Indians were being cheated out of their land and heritage, and being made into drunks and a lazy people in the process. Why they allowed it to happen escaped Other Day. Because he believed the red men were spineless, he hated them. For what white men had done to his mother and to Belle, the only woman he had ever loved, he hated them even more. While he walked, he wondered why white men had to put so much stock in their attitude toward someone different from themselves? Almost everyone he met, asked him in time if he was a half-breed. Sometimes he answered, sometimes he didn't.

When Logan neared the saloon, he stepped onto the boardwalk and walked to the door, his boots making loud clumping noises in the silence. Pushing open the door, he entered.

A haze of dust hung in the air giving the interior a fuzzy, indistinct look. Several men sat at a table in the center of the room while a few lolled at the bar, which was nothing more than a wide plank lying on top of three barrels. A whore, the center of attention for the men at the bar, ignored Other Day when he entered. Two other women sat near the men at the table.

Preferring to drink by himself, Other Day walked to the end of the bar farthest from those standing. The bartender, a small man wearing a high hat and an unkempt beard, looked at him but made no move to serve him.

After a few moments passed, the bartender finally turned and sauntered over to Other Day. "Whuskey?" he asked.

The 'breed nodded and said, "And a beer." He fixed his attention on the wall behind the bar and continued staring at it when the man brought him his drinks. He threw a $20 gold piece on the counter and picked up the beer. The first sip went down smoothly despite the fact the beer was warm. It made no difference to the 'breed since he'd had cold beer only once or twice in his life.

The bartender picked up the gold piece and whistled. "I ain't seen many of them around lately. Times is tough. Looky here, ever'body. A genuine twenty-dollar gold piece. Aint' that somethin'?"

The other patrons turned to the 'breed and looked at him as if for the first time. One of the whores who was seated stood and walked over to him.

Other Day smiled inwardly. They'd probably go nuts if they knew he had nine more like it in the hollowed-out part of his belt. He had had little chance to spend any money since leaving Hades and thought the money would last him a good long while.

"Howdy, stranger," the woman said, moving close to Other Day.

He looked down at the woman. She might have been pretty at one time, but life as a whore on the frontier had more than taken its toll and he wanted no part of her.

"You plannin' on bein' around these parts for long?" she asked. "Flea Hill could use some new faces onc't in a while. Things is mighty dull here at the Thirsty Tonsil."

The 'breed grunted. "Is that the name of this place?"

She nodded. "Just rode in, I s'pose."

"From up north and I'm riding on through. Going south, where it's warmer."

"Plenty hot here today. Should be cooler but it sure was hot today," she said. "Where you goin' south? Texas? Mexico? Where?"

"Don't rightly know. If I did, I probably wouldn't tell you anyway."

She snorted at the rebuff but continued prying. "Where you comin' from? You interested in a little party?"

Other Day looked around. The building had one floor. Where was she planning on taking him, or any other customer for that matter? Up on the roof? Or maybe right there in the saloon's lone room? He didn't know if either situation would work. He looked at the woman again and shook his head.

"What's your name, half-breed? Mine's Suellen."

He looked down at her, preferring not to explain his unusual first name, which resulted from a misunderstanding the day he was baptized. "Logan," he said matter-of-factly. "I notice there isn't a second floor on the building. Just where do you conduct your business? Mind you, I'm not interested, just curious."

"Curiosity ain't a good thing to have in these parts, Logan. But if'n you want to know—maybe for some other time—I'd take you to my house. It's down the end of the street."

Other Day grunted his understanding but said nothing.

"You sure you don't want to come on over? I'd make you feel real comfortable-like. You look like you ain't seen a bed in a long time."

Other Day didn't move away when the woman sidled in closer. He hated beds. He was just tired from riding that day and for the last how ever many days he'd been on the trail from that cesspool Hades. He didn't move when he felt her hand rubbing his thigh, moving ever closer to his crotch. He reached up and picked up the shot glass of rye whiskey. Dumping it down, he motioned for the bartender to fill the small glass again.

"Come on, honey," Suellen said, squeezing the 'breed's pants.

The bartender filled the glass and looked up at Other Day.

"Get away from me, lady," the 'breed growled.

"Say, that ain't no way to speak to her," the bartender said, looking past Other Day. "Is it, boys?"

Instantly Other Day's body reacted, the peculiar itching sensation, which warned him of impending danger, crawling over his back and chest. He steeled himself, ready for whatever the patrons of the bar were about to do. There was no way he could take on the four or five men who had been in the saloon when he entered, but he would give a good accounting of himself if they started something. If he had the opportunity to draw his .44 or the bowie knife he carried in his right boot, he would. Either one would give him a decided advantage. Of course the men in the bar could also draw their weapons. He'd have to play it the way it fell.

The half-breed sensed the men closing in on him. Suellen fell to her knees and groped more at his crotch. "Come on, big fella," she said in a whining, begging voice. "Let's you 'n me have ourselves a little party. You got lotsa money, ain'tcha?"

Other Day didn't answer the whore, and when he felt hands grabbing at him, the woman stood. But before she could move away, Logan grabbed her by the neck and threw her around, making her collide with the men to his right. At the same time, once he'd released his grip on her, his hand flew to the .44 he wore, and it fairly leaped into his hand. He cocked the gun in the same motion and brought it around to face the rest of the bar patrons. Before he completed the half-circle and gained the upper hand, a fist lashed out, striking him in the jaw. The Colt flew from his hand, discharging when it struck the floor.

Rather than going for the gun, the men closed in on the lone half-breed. They fell in on him, their weight alone bearing him to the floor. Fists pounded at him, and he felt several pointed toes of boots digging into his stomach as the men kicked at him. In the struggle Logan reached for the bowie knife through the slitted flap in his right pants leg but failed to get it. The throwing knife he wore down the back of his shirt was out of reach, and the hunting knife in his left boot was unattainable since there was no flap through which he could get it.

The hands dragged the 'breed to his feet, holding him tightly, and he couldn't move.

"We've gotta teach you some manners, mister," one of the men said. "It ain't nice to ride into a town and not pay attention to the ladies there. What say, boys? What should we teach him?"

"Just a minute, Joe," one of the men said. "You wasn't on that posse, yesterday, was you?"

"You know I wasn't."

"Well, we were lookin' for an Injun. There was one with the gang that robbed the Centralia stage. They got off with two-thousand dollars in gold."

"I knew there was a holdup. You think this half-breed is the one the driver and guard saw?"

"Bet it is." The man who had stopped Joe from teaching Other Day a lesson turned to the 'breed and said, "You rob the stage, Injun?"

Other Day said nothing. When the man stepped even closer, the 'breed lashed out with his foot, catching the man in the groin. Taken off guard, the men holding him relaxed their grip for an instant, which was all the half-breed needed. The 'breed pulled his arms together and the men followed, smashing their heads together. Groggy, they dropped to the floor.

The other two men who had confronted him, leaped forward, one behind the other and were met with a balled-up fist crashing into the jaw of the first. He fell back hard, collapsing into the arms of the man behind him. Other Day followed up his attack before the others could get the advantage.

The woman who had just gotten up off the floor, found herself being picked up again by the half-breed. He held her under her armpits, then swung her in a circle. Her high-topped shoes caught one man in the face as he was clambering to his feet, and he fell onto another man who was trying to stand.

Someone pushed Other Day from behind, and he and the woman went sprawling across the floor. When he stopped moving, his .44 was next to his right hand. Grabbing and cocking it in the same motion, he brought the gun around and leveled it at the men who were closing in on him. They all froze as if suddenly turned into statues.

"That's right, boys," Other Day said evenly. "Just back off a bit now. I'd like a chance to catch my breath and have another shot before we talk any more." In the back of his mind he remembered that his gelding was unsaddled and a block or so away at the livery stable. He had no idea how he could keep these men at bay and then get to his horse without any sort of trouble. Trouble! Why did it dog his steps? Why couldn't people just leave him alone and treat him like any other man?

"You got a marshal in town? A sheriff?" he asked.

The men stood, glaring at him, each one frowning in a surly way. No one answered. Then Suellen spoke up.

"You bet we got a sheriff. He'll be comin' in any minute. He heard your gun go off before. You're gonna get in all sorts of trouble when he hears what you did to me. He's my man. I sure wouldn't want to be in your boots when he hears how you threw me around like you did."

Other Day groaned. That was all he needed. A sheriff who had a hankering for one of the ugly fallen angels at the town's lone saloon. He thought back to his interpretation of the town's atmosphere of hopelessness. He had been right. This town was hopeless. That would be a helluva lot better name than Flea Hill.

"For your information, boys," the breed said, "I haven't robbed any stage and I earned the money I spent here. Now, if all of you will accompany me to the livery stable, I'll get my horse and be on my way. I want no trouble here. I rode in to get cleaned up, have some whiskey and a meal. That's all. You understand that, don't you?"

The men didn't answer.

Other Day followed their eyes and saw that most were watching something behind him. The only thing there was the bartender. Then his body itched. As he turned to see what the man behind the bar was about to do, something smashed into his head.

His senses reeled and his sinuses drained as the room took on a flashing purple and gold aura. Stars and pinpoints of light rippled through his vision. Half-conscious, he felt the .44 slipping from his fingers. His knees buckled and he crumbled slowly to the floor.

He could hear voices from far off but couldn't understand who was talking.

"I got his gun," one voice said.

Another, more distant voice said, "What's goin' on in here?"

"Hey, Sheriff, we got the Injun who held up the Centralia stage. Sure's got a beard for a redskin."

The sheriff moved in closer and said, "I see that. You boys are to be congratulated. I'll see to it that you get the reward if one's bein' offered."

The dazed 'breed felt hands grabbing at him and lifting him.

"Bring 'im on over to the jail. We'll lock 'im up. Judge Ostwinkle will be in town tomorrow or the next day," the sheriff said. "Once this Indian's in jail, I'll have to buy you boys a drink."

The clamour of approval was the last thing the 'breed heard as he was carried out through the door toward the jail on the other side of the street.

CHAPTER TWO

Other Day couldn't believe his eyes: two Belle Doolins rushed at him, heaving sledge hammers poised over their heads. What was wrong? Why were they attacking him? What had he done? He held up his hands to stop them but the two women, the resemblance between them so striking that anyone would believe they were twins, continued their approach. Before he could stop them or say a word, they launched their assault. The heavy hammers pounded on his head, and he wanted to scream out his pain but didn't. Instead Logan took the beating for whatever reason he thought valid.

He opened his mouth to yell—

—but nothing came out.

He squinted and shut his eyes immediately. The light was too bright. His head hurt. Had the two women actually attacked him? That was impossible. Belle Doolin was dead. He had buried her on the hillside overlooking the burned-out shell that had once been her home. Melanie Balland, the woman who looked almost exactly like Belle, was miles to the north with her father, finishing up the job of building the railroad to Hades.

It had been a dream. But why had he dreamt of something so awful? Neither Belle nor Melanie would ever have done anything such as he had just dreamt. He had best stop thinking about Belle so much. He had been doing just that when he had ridden into—

Where the hell was he? In a little nothing of a town with a strange name. What was it? Something Hill. *Flea* Hill! That was it. But where was he now?

He tried opening his eyes again and glanced around. He saw a window with bars on it. He turned his head and saw a barred door. He was in jail. Where? In Flea Hill? Of course. In the two-storied building with Courthouse on a sign in front. The only decent-looking building in town other than the railroad depot, which stood next door. Logan swung his legs off the bunk on which he lay and stood. The room spun about for a moment and he swayed. Gradually the 'breed regained his balance and went to the window.

He had been in jails before but nothing like this one. The cell was on the second floor. That in itself wasn't good. From what he could see outside, there was nothing on the wall that would help him get down if he could figure a way to get through the bars or pull one of them out. He turned and stepped off the cell. It was big: 20 feet by ten with three bunks on each side of the two short walls and six on the long. On the other side of the bars, a narrow hallway ran the length of the cell and ended at the blank wall. The wall parallel to the bars was an interior wall. To his right, a door was the only sign of an opening of any sort, other than the window in the cell.

He hadn't paid much attention to the building and took the time to visualize it in his mind. It was a combination stone and brick building and appeared relatively new compared with the buildings that lined the opposite side of the street. They were all dumps, appearing to have been built in a slipshod manner. Why then, had such a sturdy jail and courthouse been built in Flea Hill? Perhaps it was a sign of better times to come for the ramshackle village.

Whatever the reason, Other Day found himself inside the building, locked in what appeared to be the only cell.

Suddenly he realized that his boots weren't on. He looked about quickly and saw them lying near the bunk on which he had awakened. When he picked up the right one, he knew the bowie knife he carried in the specially designed built-in sheath was gone. So was the hunting knife Logan carried in the left one. Reaching behind his neck he groped for the throwing blade he carried there. It too was gone, along with its sheath. He had not been stripped of all his weapons in a long time. So long a time in fact, he couldn't remember the last time he had been completely weaponless. Undoubtedly, his .44 was in the possession of the sheriff. He recalled hearing somebody greet the lawman before losing consciousness.

Other Day frowned. There had been something else he had heard before he passed out completely from the blow to his head. The men in the bar had decided he had been involved in a stage holdup someplace. Then everything had gone black and he had awakened there in the jail cell.

The only advantage he could see he had right then was the fact that he was in the cell alone. It was apparent that the townspeople planned on holding more than one prisoner at a time considering the 12 bunks hanging from the walls. Luckily for the 'breed, he could pace about trying to devise a plan to get out of the situation in which he found himself. If the room had 11 other prisoners in it, he'd go crazy in a matter of minutes. He hated confined spaces, he hated crowds, and most of all, he hated the buildings that whites felt were so important. How could they possibly want to live, sleep, and eat inside all of the time? He tolerated saloons and restaurants on occasion because those places usually had higher ceilings and didn't seem to press in on him. He looked at the ceiling of the cell. It was at most nine or ten feet high. Any lower and he'd be screaming for his freedom.

Logan paced about the room, a low growl rumbling deep within his chest. When he passed the window, he stopped and looked outside for a long while. He absently ran a finger over his face, lingering for a moment on the z-shaped scar that marked his countenance.

Railroad tracks, wider apart than the three-foot

gauge line he had been hired to act as troubleshooter for up north, ran past the building. Another track lay beyond it. Logan could tell that the farther track was the mainline because the rails were shinier, whereas the other track, which had rusted a little, was a siding. To Other Day's right, a short water tank stood on the far side of the rails, and he could see that it had no roof on it. Beyond it, a windmill, its fan turning in a squeaking rhythm, pumped water from a well for the tank. A huge pile of wood near the water supply told him the engine stopped in Flea Hill for fuel. Almost directly in front of him, on the opposite side of the tracks, was an outhouse. It might belong to the courthouse and jail. Unless the half-breed figured a way out of the cell on his own, he would have to be taken outside to relieve himself sooner or later. He might have a chance then.

He wondered what time it was. How long had he been in jail? His stomach rumbled and he wanted food of some sort.

Just then, the door opened and a tall, heavyset man walked into the hallway outside the barred room.

"You're awake," he said. "I'm Sheriff Ivo Turner."

"Why am I in here, Sheriff?" Other Day asked, eyeing the star on the man's wool shirt.

"That's a dumb question. You robbed the Centralia stage."

"I did, huh? You saw me do it?"

"No, I didn't see you do it, you half-breed sonofabitch. The driver and guard told us."

"They said I robbed them? Is that right? Just what did they say?"

"That some white men and an Injun robbed 'em."

"And because I am what I am, I'm the Indian that did it, huh?"

"All you redskins look alike to me."

"How was he dressed? In white man's clothes like me? What kind of horse did he ride? Did they see his face?"

"How the hell should I know? They said an Injun did it and I got an Injun in my jail. That takes care of that."

"'You called me a half-breed. I am half Pawnee and half white. And you still think I did it?"

"Hell, yes. It don't make any difference to me. Like I said, you Injuns all look alike to most folks, anyhow."

"Where are my weapons? And my belt? Where's my belt?"

"Oh, yeah," the sheriff said and chuckled. "They're nice and safe. Took your belt so you wouldn't have a weapon. I never seen so much iron and metal come off of one man before. You were a regular walkin' butcher shop, weren't you, 'breed? Where'd you get the bowie? I ain't seen one before. One of the old timers at the Thirsty Tonsil told me what it was. I've heard of 'em but never seen one. Where'd you get it?"

"I got it from a priest a long time ago." Other Day thought back to the time Father McGhee had given it to him, more as a memento of a by-gone era than a weapon. Other Day had worked with the knife and had become adept at using the large weapon. In a short time, he learned to throw it with almost as much accuracy as he threw with a regular knife. The blade had tasted a man's blood on more than one occasion.

"Well, you won't be using it much anymore."

"I don't understand."

"Well, we got you dead to rights for holdin' up the stage. If you should get off that, we'll get you for horse stealin'."

"What?" Other Day charged the barred doors and reached out for the sheriff. The lawman ducked out of the way and grinned at him. "I've never stolen a horse in my life." The 'breed growled the words.

"That ain't what Jake Schuster says. He says your horse is just like a geldin' someone stole from him a while back."

"How long ago? How long ago did he have it stolen?"

"He didn't say nothin' exact. Just that it was taken like he said. I believe him though. Ol' Jake never lies, that I know of."

Other Day shook his head. He was in a fix, all right. The sheriff had a brain the size of a pebble and was ready, willing, and able to hand him over to a judge and jury. He'd have to figure out some way to escape from the cell and Flea Hill. He had no weapons, he had no horse, and he was locked up in a cell on the second floor of what appeared to be a very secure jail. He had problems.

He looked at Turner. "So what happens next, Sheriff?"

"Judge Ostwinkle is due in tomorrow on the

train. You'll go before 'im and the trial time'll be set. Probably for some time that same afternoon or the next day at the latest. He don't like to mess around long on cases like yours."

"What time do I eat or don't I?"

"What kind o' question is that? 'Course you're gonna eat. My deputy is over gettin' it at the cafe now."

As if to confirm the sheriff's statement, Other Day looked toward the door when he heard footsteps approaching from the other side.

"Get over against the wall, 'breed," Turner said, drawing his six-gun.

As Other Day obliged and stood near the window, the door to the cell area opened. A short, stocky man backed through the door, carrying a tray covered with a red-and-white checkered cloth. When he turned, his eyes locked with Logan's for a moment and then the 'breed's attention dropped to the man's sidearm. A .44 Army revolver was stuck in the holster he wore.

"Stay put, outlaw," the newcomer said, looking to Turner to protect him when he entered the cell with the food.

"Right, Injun. Don't move from where you are." Turner cocked his six-gun and levelled it at Other Day.

Other Day turned to look out the window. Such fools. The sun had dropped behind the hills ringing the town, and an early dusk was rapidly settling across the valley floor to the south. The 'breed stared out at the open expanse. He'd give anything if he could be out there right then, breathing the air of freedom.

"All right, Injun, you can turn around now," Turner said when the cell door clanked shut.

Other Day turned and saw the tray sitting on his bunk. Choosing to ignore the sheriff and his deputy, he walked over to the food and sat down. When he uncovered it, he found a thin stew with a few potatoes and carrots forlornly lying on a tin plate. Two pieces of meat the size of his thumbnail hid behind one of the potatoes. A piece of thick bread that looked as if it might be moldy and a cup of cold coffee finished the menu. A wooden spoon was the only utensil they gave him. They had thought of everything by not giving him a chance to have a weapon in the form of a knife or fork accidentally put in his hands.

"Did he admit to the holdup, Sheriff?" the deputy asked.

"Naw. You know how these Injuns are, Jake. They don't say much when they're caught red-handed."

"That's sorta funny, Sheriff," Jake said and laughed.

Other Day wondered if the man was the same Jake who the sheriff said claimed the bay gelding as his. He asked.

The sheriff said, "Yup. He's the one all right and he's much obliged to you for bringing him back in good shape. Right, Jake?"

"I always liked that there horse."

Other Day glared at him. Why protest? They wouldn't listen to anything he had to say, no matter what he said.

"When you get finished with your grub, we'll take you outside to the outhouse for your evenin' visitation."

Other Day showed no reaction, but he knew he just might have a chance when that happened. He nodded slowly and picked up the wooden spoon. The food was terrible—bland, undercooked, and tough as jerky.

"We're goin' downstairs right now, but we'll come git you in a while. Be ready." The sheriff holstered his six-gun and followed the deputy to the door.

When he was alone, Other Day dipped the bread in the thin gravy and ate. Then he went to the window to study the lay of the land to see if there might be a place he could use to his advantage when they took him to the outhouse. From where he was, he could see nothing. Perhaps it would be different once he got down to the ground. For all he knew there was another outhouse someplace close by, and the one he could see didn't even belong to the courthouse.

Turning he went back to the food tray and carried it to the opposite side of the cell. Rolling back the thin blanket on the middle bunk, he emptied the remainder of his meal and covered it up. He didn't want anything said about his not appreciating their food.

Just as he returned to his own bunk, the door opened and the sheriff and Jake returned.

"Okay, Injun," the sheriff said, "put your hands inside your pants and come out when I tell you to. Understand?"

Other Day nodded and thrust his hands inside his pants at the waist. He wondered if Turner had found the gold pieces tucked into the secret pouch of his pants belt.

"Now come out once the door is open." Jake went to the barred door and unlocked it.

When Turner motioned for him to come out, Other Day stepped forward, his hands tucked inside his waistline. If he tried anything, he would telegraph his intentions by having to lift his arms to get his hands out in the open. With both men behind him, he'd be gunned down in the back before he could hope to do something to gain his freedom. Turner was no fool. Then too neither was he.

They walked down a broad flights of steps toward the first floor. When they reached it, Other Day hesitated, not knowing which way to go.

"Turn to yer right and go back along the stairway, Injun. We'll tell you where to go from there," Turner said.

Other Day did as he was told and walked along the narrow passageway that led to the rear of the building.

"To your right now and then to your left," Turner said. "Then you'll see a door. Jake'll open it for you."

Other Day followed the man's simple instructions and saw the door when he turned the second time.

"Hold it," Turner said and the deputy stepped around Other Day.

The 'breed wanted to throw his body against the deputy and make a break for the door. Instead, he decided to wait until he'd seen the entire lay of the area behind the courthouse. Apparently they were headed toward the outhouse across the tracks, the same one he'd seen from the cell window. It was getting dark and he knew they'd have to take him to the same place sometime the next morning. He might have a better opportunity then.

Even though there wasn't much difference in the air inside the cell and behind the building, the half-breed recognized the scent of freedom—it was a smell he loved.

They crossed the two tracks and Other Day walked directly to the outhouse. Inside, flies upset by his entering buzzed about, and the stench overwhelmed the 'breed. White men had the most peculiar ideas about sanitation. There were much better ways to do the same thing. When he finished, he rapped on the door as he had been instructed and the door was opened.

Once outside, he filled his lungs with the unpolluted air. It tasted sweet after the rancid stink he'd been subject to, and he inhaled deeply several times.

As he returned to the courthouse, he studied the area to his right. The railroad depot sat on the same side of the tracks as the building toward which he was walking. A distance of 200 feet separated the two structures.

After crossing the tracks the three men re-entered the building and Other Day was taken upstairs and put in the cell.

After the two lawmen left, Other Day lay down on the bunk and stared at the ceiling. He was not in a good situation. He had no idea what would happen once the judge arrived. If the judge was a fair man, Other Day might be given a chance. If he wasn't, the 'breed would have more problems confronting him.

He wanted to be free, outside under the open

sky. He hated where he was. Maybe he might dream of Belle again. If it was the same sort of dream he had had before he awoke after being knocked out, he wanted no part of it. Belle would not have hurt him—nor would Melanie for that matter.

He rolled over on his side and stared at the wall that was only a few inches away. He cursed his luck and closed his eyes. He would sleep and then confront his problem after he awoke.

He clenched his fists for a moment and then relaxed as he fell asleep.

CHAPTER THREE

Other Day sat up on his bunk, his eyes wide, every sense tingling. What was that noise he'd just heard? Then it came again. A train whistle. The train was coming into Flea Hill.

The 'breed leaped from the bunk and went to the window. He could see nothing yet but the blasting sound of steam grew louder as the engine and its train drew nearer. Another blast of the whistle—a loud, shrieking scream—rent the predawn stillness, and then Other Day could see it.

The locomotive, its high-wheeled drivers slowing as it approached the water tank, gradually came to a stop, its tender directly under the spout. Excess steam blasted from the cylinder cocks, sending up a loud hiss that sounded like every rattlesnake for miles around had gathered in Flea Hill.

Then, as the cloud of steam grew, Other Day saw the figure of a man coming through the white haze. Tall, gaunt-looking in the early light of day, the man strode confidently toward the courthouse. Two other people carrying bags approached the train from the direction of the depot to board it.

Just as the steam stopped and completely dissipated, the 'breed could see a man on the tender pulling down the water spout. A rush of water flowed out, and captivated by the sight, Other Day didn't hear the cell door open.

"All right, you. Come on," Sheriff Turner said. "The judge is here and wants to see you."

Other Day whirled around to face the sheriff and his deputy. Now? Before breakfast? Before the sun was even up? The judge probably was a hanging judge and loved his work enough to want to start proceedings against him quickly.

"No breakfast?" the 'breed asked. "Now?"

"You got a problem understanding what I just said, Injun?" Turner asked.

His deputy, Jake Schuster, glowered and took a menacing step toward the prisoner, but stopped when Other Day did the same to him.

"I have no problem, Sheriff. But isn't it a bit unusual to got to court before the sun's even up?"

"Not necessarily. The judge'll only be here for a few hours. The westbound train comes from Promise City around noon and he'll probably want to be on it."

"You mean I'm going to be tried before noon?"

"You bet, Redskin. Judge Ostwinkle ain't one to fool around none." Turner motioned for Other Day to come out of the cell. "More than likely, you'll be swingin' by dinnertime."

Other Day shook his head and stepped forward. He had to think fast and do something quick, or he'd be doing just what the sheriff had suggested. When Logan was within a step of the door, the sheriff and deputy drew and held their six-guns on him.

"Just walk real nice and don't make no trouble, Injun, and everythin'll be all right. And keep your hands up. Understan'?" Turner waved his gun in a menacing way. "And leave your hat there on the bunk."

In way of answering, Other Day raised his hands to shoulder height and walked slowly toward the door that led to the wide staircase.

"Any chance of going outside for a minute to ease my gut, Sheriff?"

"Whatcha mean?"

"He wants to take a piss," Schuster said grinning.

"No, sir," Turner said. "The judge is probably waitin' in the courtroom right now. You can do that later."

Other Day shrugged and started down the stairs. When he reached the bottom, he turned and said, "Which way now?"

"That-a-way," Turner said, motioning with his gun toward a set of doors on the left.

Other Day walked toward them and opened the door. The tall, gaunt man he'd seen from the cell window stood near the high desk that served for a bench, rifling through a stack of papers. He turned and glared at Other Day.

The 'breed returned the stare, concluding the

judge was not a humorous man and would probably go along with whatever the sheriff wanted. Other Day had to figure something out soon or his days would soon be over. Maybe that would be the smart thing to do—let the town law of Flea Hill finish him. His discontent with the world and mankind in general would be quieted once and for all. Even though he'd found solace in killing the man responsible for his mother's death and again when he practically tore the head off the man who had raped and killed Belle Doolin, he'd found no peace of mind after his sense of justice and revenge had been satisfied. Would he ever find any peace of mind in his roamings? If he could find one person who understood him, he'd feel as if there might be hope for him. Still, if he stayed there in Flea Hill his life would be ended.

Then he thought of Father David McGhee. He was the one man he had ever met, who seemed to understand completely Other Day Logan's thoughts and actions. He would not despair now and accept an unfair end to his life. He was innocent of the crime with which Sheriff Ivo Turner had charged him. He would ask the judge to accept his story and hope that the justice of the court was fair in its dealings.

"Just stand there and don't make no noise, Injun," Turner said. He approached the bench after the judge had seated himself and said, "Your honor, this here Injun is guilty of holdin' up the Centralia stage a few days ago. He stole my deputy's horse and should have his neck stretched."

Instead of reprimanding the sheriff for his colored, one-sided presentation of the situation, the judge turned his attention from the lawman and glared at the 'breed.

"How do you plead, Injun?" Judge Ostwinkle asked in a gruff voice.

Other Day looked up at him. He seldom, if ever, had to prove that any of his actions were right when others accused him of doing wrong. Usually something happened or presented itself that would set the record straight. But this time, for some reason, he felt he should plead his innocence and try to buy time. At least he felt he was in no immediate danger since his peculiar itching sensation had not yet bothered him. Maybe he would be all right if he followed the judge's lead and the legal procedures.

"I'm innocent, your honor."

Ostwinkle grunted and turned to the sheriff. "You go round up a jury and we'll get this little business over and done with before the noon train comes in. Don't pick anybody who might want to argue the point about this here Injun's innocence. Understand?"

Turner nodded, faced Other Day and said to Schuster, "Take him on back up to the cell, Jake. I'll go start poundin' on doors to get a jury together."

"I'd still like to go out—" Other Day said.

The shrill whistle of the steam engine, getting ready to leave, cut off his last words.

"What'd he say?" the judge asked, addressing the sheriff once more.

"What'd you say, Injun?"

"He said he had to go outside and piss," the deputy said and grinned again.

"All right." Turner motioned with his head toward the rear of the building and turned his back on Other Day as Jake Schuster drove him out of the courtroom with the muzzle of his six-gun.

Other Day, his hands still held at shoulder height, knew he had to do something and do it faster than the swift arm of justice moved in Flea Hill. The judge was obviously as eager to be over and done with the situation as Turner, and he was probably just as convinced that it should go in the direction the sheriff had suggested.

Schuster prodded him in the back with the barrel of his .44 army revolver, and Other Day moved toward the double doors. He walked slowly through them, then toward the passageway along the broad set of stairs that led to the second floor. If Other Day was going to do something, he had to do it right then or he'd never have the chance again. There'd be too many people around later when the trial started.

Just as he started down the passageway, he spun around, his left hand balled into a fist, and caught Schuster completely off guard, smashing him in the right side of the face and nose. Blood spurted from his nose, and the startled deputy stood still for a moment, dazed, appearing as if he were not quite certain as to what had happened. His .44 tipped forward before Schuster fell back.

Other Day wheeled about and ran down the passageway to the first turn, and headed around the second turn, and dashed for the back of the building toward the door to freedom. Outside, the train whistle screamed once more.

His mind set on gaining his freedom, Other Day quickly put together a plan. He had to beat the train and get to the opposite side of the tracks. If it stopped at the depot, he'd never have a chance to escape. He had to get across the tracks before the train cut off that path. The train had taken on water and probably fuel during its stop. The judge had gotten off as soon as the train had stopped and a couple of passengers had gotten on. The train had to be on its way. If it weren't—Other Day didn't want to think of catching a bullet in his back as he ran away from the so-called law of Flea Hill.

When Other Day reached the back door, he heard Schuster crying out for him to stop. Because of the jog in the corridor, the deputy couldn't fire at Logan until he reached the back door. By the time that happened, the 'breed hoped he would have the moving train between him and the courthouse.

Bursting through the door, he saw the locomotive picking up speed, its long, pointed cowcatcher almost to the line of the door. The 'breed ran as hard as he could, first across the siding track, then for the main line itself. When the half-breed dived in front of the train, the pilot just missed him, and he landed on his shoulder, completed a somersault, and landed on his feet, running.

A gunshot from behind struck the cowcatcher and Other Day relaxed for a moment. He thought he heard the deputy yelling at the train to stop, but the racket of the puffing steam engine all but drowned him out. The locomotive continued picking up speed and for that Other Day was thankful. For, as long as the train was passing by, he would have time to climb aboard and be on his way. He only hoped the deputy wouldn't do the same thing.

Just as he was about to reach out and take one of the grabirons, he saw the water tank and recalled it had no roof. Opting to do the unexpected, he ran full tilt toward the tank and the ladder that rose to the top on the side away from the track and the courthouse.

Clambering up, hand over hand, foot over foot, he reached the top just as the last car, a nondescript caboose, passed the tank. Going up and over, Other Day lowered himself partially into the water. It was cold but would heat up during the day as the sun rose higher in the sky. The train whistled again, covering the sound of any splashing that Schuster might hear above the rumbling cars.

The 'breed listened intently for the sound of voices but heard none. Then, as if in answer to his inquisitiveness, he heard the voice of Sheriff Ivo Turner call out.

"Jake musta climbed on board, too. He'll get that goddamned Injun 'cause he ain't got no gun or knife. We have them in my office." He laughed and was joined in the odd merriment by Judge Earl Ostwinkle.

Then Ostwinkle yelled, "You'd better get on that train, too, just to make sure the Injun don't get away. I ain't hung one in a long time."

Because he heard nothing else, Other Day assumed that Turner was chasing the train. He had to risk taking a look. Pulling himself up so that his eyes were level with the edge of the top, he smiled when he saw Turner running after the last car of the mixed freight and passenger train. After a long chase, the sheriff pulled himself up onto the rear platform of the caboose.

Other Day looked down at his feet. The water had lowered when the train filled its tender. He had been able to see the level from the cell window. Now it was almost three feet lower.

He gently eased himself down until nothing but his shoulders were out of the water. He stoically bore the discomfort of the chilly feeling. He hoped the sun would soon rise high enough in the sky to start warming the tank.

The sound of squeaking floated through the early morning quiet. The windmill! Someone had opened it so that the wind would turn the fan and the pump could refill the tank. Suddenly the splash of water sounded in the round container, and Other Day knew he would be able to be seen from the cell window if the water rose too high. Of course Turner and Schuster would have to think to look out the cell window and see him. But for some reason, he felt the two would probably conclude he had jumped from the train when they weren't looking and had gotten away.

Now, the 'breed would wait until dark, then get the hell out of Flea Hill. He thought that Bell's Town had been bad before he took care of Ike Furlong by killing him along with Ace Hanlon and the rest of the troublemakers. Mr. Eulberg and the other merchants had been grateful to him but he had left. And now, Logan was positive he didn't want to stay in Flea Hill for any reason.

He looked around at the circular confines of the wet prison. He had gotten out of jail only to find himself in another one. But this one was of his own choosing. Once the sun was down, he'd leave.

CHAPTER FOUR

The 'breed hung onto the top of the wooden tank and watched the water flowing into the tank. He wondered if the tank was ever allowed to overflow. If it were, his head would be exposed above the line of the tank and someone might see him. As the wind blew and died, the water flowed and ebbed. At that rate, it would take a long time for the water, which was almost three feet from the top, to overflow. The tank itself was about 18 feet across. As he floated, Other Day remembered that he had wanted to get a bath, a shave, and a hot meal when he came to Flea Hill. Well, he'd gotten one out of the three.

His stomach growled. He was hungry, but he knew that he would not be able to do anything about it until well after dark.

Off to one side, near the top, he saw two pieces

of strap iron that held the tank together on the outside, sticking through to the interior of the structure. His feet telegraphed an idea to his brain and he struggled to get his boots off. If he hung them up on the strap iron they might dry some before he had to leave his sanctuary.

After the boots were hung up, he wiggled his toes and felt relieved. Logan floated on his back, looking up at the sky. The sun beat down on him, and from its position he knew his head was toward the courthouse. Deciding to reconnoiter the area, he swam to one side and pulled himself up on the creosoted planks that made up the sides of the reservoir. He clung to the four inch-thick boards and eased himself up until he could see the buildings of Flea Hill.

The town appeared as dead as it had been when he rode in. He looked down the tracks to his left and then to his right. He narrowed his eyes and studied the parallel threads of iron that seemed to meet in the hazy distance. Two men were walking along the rails toward Flea Hill. He watched intently and, as the men drew closer, he could see that Sheriff Ivo Turner and Deputy Jake Schuster were returning to Flea Hill, but without their prisoner.

The 'breed smiled to himself. If he had gotten on the train, as had been his first inclination, he might very well be walking with them. But the sight of the tank had changed his plans and now, unless Turner or Schuster were considerably more intelligent than Other Day thought them to be, he'd be safe until dark.

Whipping off his red headband, he thrust it in

his pocket. Someone might see that bit of color when he thrust his head over the top of the tank. Pulling himself up to the top once more, he watched as the two lawmen walked, without once looking at the tank or anything else for that matter, directly to the courthouse and entered through the back door.

Shortly thereafter, the whistle for the westbound train, heading in the opposite direction from the one that had come to town earlier that morning, wailed across the hot plain.

Again, Other Day pulled himself up to watch the train come into town, but backed off when he heard a door slam. Carefully looking over the edge, he saw the sheriff and Judge Ostwinkle come out through the same door he'd used to make his escape that morning. They headed directly toward the station. The Judge was leaving town since there wasn't any business for him in Flea Hill.

The puffing of the locomotive as it wheezed into the station area grew loud and Other Day relaxed. The noise would be paramount for the time being, and if he did make any sound, no one would hear it.

The engine sounded so close that the 'breed was tempted to cover his ears because of the noise. An earsplitting scream sounded and was quickly followed by the gushing of water. He heard the words, "—much to fill the tank," and then he realized what was happening. The engine crew was filling the engine's tank with water.

Seconds later, he felt the tug of the whirlpool setting up as the water drained from the tank. What if the water got down too low and the wind didn't blow enough to raise the level to the point where he could grasp the top? He'd really be a prisoner in a jail of his own making then. Maybe he should grab the top while he still could. But could he hang on till dark without the water to buoy him?

No sooner had those thoughts crossed his mind than he heard the loud shrieking again as the water spout was returned to its upright position. The pull of the water flow stopped and Other Day appraised the situation. The water had lowered no more than half a foot. Unless there were a lot more trains coming through, which he doubted, the trickle of water that maintained itself would replace some of the lost level, and he would be able to leave when he wanted.

A few minutes later, the train whistled and left the station. Other Day went to one side of the tank and pulled himself up to watch the train gradually disappear in the distance.

He looked at the sun and calculated that it was early afternoon. He settled back to wait. His patience could be long in certain situations and this was one such case.

The sun had been down for almost two hours when the 'breed decided to make his move to escape from Flea Hill. The full moon rode low on the eastern horizon as he pulled himself up near where his boots hunt on the strap iron. They had dried and were stiff but not unyielding. A little wear would have them as good as they had been before their untimely dunking. Balancing on the edge of the tank side, Other Day pulled the boots free, and, with them tucked under one arm, slowly made his way down the ladder. When he was in the deep shadows at the foot of the tank's upright supports, he sat down and pulled on his boots.

When he stood, he tried them to see if they might squeak, but found that the leather was not very stiff. Like a shadow, the 'breed made his way toward the back of the courthouse. Around on the side, through a window, he could see Schuster asleep at the desk, his feet free of boots. The only illumination, a single coal-oil lamp, burned low but lighted the interior of the office sufficiently to allow the 'breed to see that the deputy was alone. Turner was probably sleeping in a bed someplace.

When he moved away from the window, something glinted on the desk and caught Other Day's attention. He returned and peered inside. His three knives lay on the desk, the blades snapped off at the hafts. An involuntary growl escaped his lips and he moved off into the night. He hadn't seen his .44 anyplace and the only thing he wanted now was to get out of Flea Hill. The lawman had had no right to destroy what was his. Logan hadn't been found guilty of anything although he knew that, given half a chance, Turner could have proven anything he wanted to prove, as long as he could lie about it.

Other Day's last hope lay in the fact that his bay gelding might be at the livery stable, otherwise he'd be without a mount as well. The fact that the law officers had lied about the animal belonging to Schuster didn't bother him right then. From what little he had seen of Schuster, the half-breed could tell he was pretty rough around the edges, a bad actor. Other Day felt confident that the bay would not have taken a liking to him. On the other side of the coin, the gelding liked Other Day. Once he had the horse, the bay would have to be quiet while leaving Flea Hill. He didn't even want to think that his Winchester might not be with his saddle.

Without making a sound, Other Day walked the length of the only street in Flea Hill and approached the livery stable. It was on the far end of the town, but he could remedy that by riding around town. His first concern was the old man who had taken the bay when he first arrived in Flea Hill. Was he around? Did he sleep in the stable as Dick Trent did in Bell's Town?

Just as the thought of Belle Dollin was about to surface, the 'breed shook his head and drove it back to the dark corners of his memory.

When he stood at the door to the barn, he carefully lifted the latch on the half door and opened it slowly, pushing up to keep the weight off the hinges. His eyes fully adjusted to the darkness in a few seconds, and he stepped forward to begin his search for the bay gelding.

He didn't have far to look, because the animal was in the first stall. Other Day talked quietly, gently to the horse and was answered in kind by a soft whicker. As if sensing the man's intensity, the bay quieted and let the 'breed slip the bridle over his head. Other Day breathed a sigh of relief when he found the Winchester in its boot and then saddled his horse.

Backing him out of the stall, the 'breed led him

to the doorway, which he'd left open. Once outside, he mounted the horse and walked him toward the railroad tracks. He'd go south for a while, then more to the west, the direction he'd been going when he first came across Flea Hill.

At least the horse was rested, and despite his own lack of sleep, Other Day knew he could rest in the saddle if necessary. The horse would continue walking while the 'breed slept, so they could cover a lot of miles. He wanted a lot of distance between him and Flea Hill before the sun came up and the gelding's absence was reported.

The bay walked through the night, his head held high, the full moon appearing to follow along the route. Other Day caught some snatches of sleep but his senses remained alert for anything out of the ordinary.

Two hours before dawn, the gelding crossed the crest of a saddleback and started down. Some deep, innate alarm went off in the brain of the 'breed and he snapped awake, every sense at full capacity. His warning system wasn't bothering him, but he nevertheless awoke and instantly pulled back on the reins of the horse.

Below, bathed in the early morning full moon's light, a large cluster of buildings spread before him. The barns, corrals and other buildings of a large ranch stood out on the otherwise barren countryside like barbs on wire.

As best as he could estimate, Logan had ridden some 20 miles since leaving Flea Hill. He had no idea if this ranch was in the domain of Sheriff Ivo Turner or if he had ridden into another state or territory. What difference? With a little luck, he might get a job and build another stake. Turner had his money. He'd circle the ranch and come in from the opposite side the next morning when someone would see him ride in.

A strand of hair fell across his face and he brushed it back. When his hand touched his hair, the 'breed realized he hadn't put his headband back on. He reached for it but stopped. It might be better if he didn't dress exactly as he had when he was in Flea Hill. If Logan changed his appearance, he might be able to fool anyone who came searching for him from that manure pile of a town. Aside from the few people who had been in the saloon when he had gotten into trouble, the 'breed had just four men to worry about: the sheriff, his deputy, the old man at the livery stable, and the judge who had left Flea Hill for the time being. If he had a knife he could cut his hair, and without the headband no one would recognize him as the same man.

After circling the ranch, he stopped at a stream and hobbled the horse. Too bad Turner had found his knives. Cutting his hair would be a lot easier with them. Fumbling in the pre-dawn light, he found a couple of rocks rounded off from the action of the water and, holding the largest one in his left hand, struck the top with the other. A flake fell off in his hand. Not satisfied, he repeated the action and a large sliver of rock tumbled to the ground. The 'breed picked it up and examined it. One edge was razor sharp where it had been severed from the rock. An uncommon smile crossed his lips. His mother had taught him well.

Reaching up, he took a handful of his black hair

and sliced through it with the improvised knife blade. Ten minutes later, his hair, which had hung to his shoulders, didn't touch the collar of his shirt.

When he finished, he took out a couple of pieces of jerky to quiet his stomach. After he finished, he lay down and closed his eyes.

An hour later, Other Day got up. After splashing water in his face to freshen himself, he took a long drink and then unhobbled the gelding. Mounting the horse, he turned him in the direction of the ranch.

Once the buildings were in sight, he slowed and took in the sight in one sweeping glance. There was activity at the bunk house, off to his right. Several of the hands had spent the night on the ground outside. That wasn't uncommon. Whenever he'd hired on as a ranch hand, he'd often slept outside because he hated the constricting confines of a small building.

A screen door slamming brought his attention around to his left. The main house, a compact, one-story structure, sat apart from the rest of the buildings and was further separated by a brook that ran past it. A tall man, taller than Other Day, strode away from the house, across a small foot-bridge, and toward the awakening hired hands. He had to be the boss, the man who did the hiring. Other Day nudged the gelding in the sides with his heels and rode toward the ranch.

CHAPTER FIVE

"Who the hell are you?" the tall man asked, looking up at the 'breed who sat on his bay.

"Name's Logan. I just rode in from the west. I'm out of money and could sure use a job. Got anything?"

The man studied the dark-complected rider confronting him. "Where'd you come from?"

Other Day motioned with his head behind him toward the north. "I've been sleeping on the ground for most of the last month. How about that job?"

The man hesitated, then slowly nodded. "Can you break a horse? Gentle one if need be?"

Other Day smiled inwardly. He knew how to break and gentle a horse but he wouldn't do it so that he betrayed his Indian heritage. The Comanches had taught him how to break a horse and Other Day knew well that most ranch riders would give a lot to have a mount gentled by an Indian. He slowly nodded. "How many you got to break?"

"Right now just one, but you and a couple of others could ride out and bring in more for the remuda."

Other Day didn't want to ask how much it would pay. He knew it wouldn't be much over 30 dollars a month, and he'd been paid five dollars a head to break horses in the past. But he felt he could build a stake of sorts if he stayed on the ranch and didn't have anyplace to spend it. "You hired yourself a hand, Mr.—?"

"Jarting. Josiah Jarting. Go on over to the house and my daughter'll give you instructions."

"Your daughter?" Other Day wondered if she might be the foreman.

"Yeah. The foreman is out on the range with a few other hands. She'll tell you where to bunk and show you where to put your horse." Jarting turned and strode away.

Other Day turned the gelding toward the house and tied him at a rail on the near side of the brook. He walked across the footbridge and was met by a tall, rawboned woman coming out of the side door. She was every bit as tall as the 'breed, and he stared at her golden blonde hair that hung to her shoulders.

"Howdy," she said, her voice soft.

"Morning, Miss Jarting," Logan said, reaching up to tip his Stetson and then remembered it was gone. He grinned sheepishly.

"My name is Mary Ann Hyburger. Josiah is my

stepfather," she said curtly, as if to say, I'll tell you this one time but don't make the same mistake again.

Sensing the air of hostility in her voice, he forced a rare smile and said, "Sorry, Miss Hyburger. I had no idea."

"Of course, you didn't," she said more softly, as she had spoken at first. "What did he hire you for?"

"To break some horses and round up some new ones for your remuda."

"Pay's thirty dollars a month and you get paid at the end of each month. Considering it's almost the end of the month, you won't have much coming. You can find a bunk at the bunkhouse over there," she said, pointing to the building where he'd seen several hands milling around when he had ridden into the ranch proper. "Report to Gus Runde since John Henry is out on the range."

Other Day looked at her quizzically.

"John Henry Lutehoser, our foreman. What's your name?"

"Logan."

"You got a first handle?"

"Logan's enough," he said, rather than tell her his correct name. If she asked about it, he'd have to tell her how he got his first name in a baptism mix-up and that he was a half-breed. Then word would get out and the story might get back to Flea Hill to the sheriff and the deputy, who would come after him to finish what they had started.

"Playing it tight to your vest for some reason? The law after you?" she asked.

"Not that I know of. I'll anwer to Logan."

"Fine by me, Logan. You'd better get to work. Josiah doesn't like to see the hands not doing their jobs."

Other Day nodded and saluted with his right forefinger touching the brim of his nonexistent Stetson.

Two days later, Other Day hadn't broken any horses. Instead, he had been told to clean the corral of manure first. He thought it a good idea since he would be landing in it if he got thrown. When he heard the steady beat of a horse's hooves nearing, he looked up and saw a lone rider approaching from the east. Something about the man on horseback seemed familiar. When he realized it was Sheriff Ivo Turner, he turned and headed for the barn. There was manure in there to get out as well. He'd been waiting until he could drive the wagon he was using to haul the livestock refuse closer to the barn door, and now seemed like an excellent time to start inside.

From the shadowy interior of the barn, he watched Turner head his mount toward Josiah Jarting, who went to greet the visitor. What could the lawman want? Was he looking for him? He wished he was closer to the pair so he could hear what they were talking about. Then, as if to comply with the 'breed's wishes, they turned and headed toward the barn.

The two men walked side by side and entered through another door. Other Day looked around. He could go outside, but he might be caught out there if the two left without his knowing they were coming. He'd be better off staying where he was since he'd be able to keep an eye on them and perhaps an ear on what they said. Other Day moved without making a sound toward the two men, hidden by a pile of hay that lay between him and them. The 'breed stopped moving and barely breathed, listening intently.

On the other side of the haystack, Jarting sat back on a box and looked at Turner. "What do you have to report?" he asked.

"It came off without a hitch," Turner answered.

"That's good. How much?"

"A little over two thousand dollars."

"Where is it? In the usual place?" Jarting asked.

"Yep, I'll give it to you the next time you're in town. You know, I think this is gonna work. The more I think on it, the more I like it. You're a pretty smart man, Mister Jarting."

Jarting snorted at the compliment. "Of course it'll work. The government didn't pay anything for it and when I make my offer after the Injuns are run off, they'll snap it up. Then my spread'll be the biggest around, and I can double the size of my herd."

Turner laughed. "The best part is, by havin' everybody think the redskins held up the stage and are pullin' some of these other robberies, it'll be all the more convincin'. You'll never guess what I almost had for you."

After a short pause, Jarting snapped, "I don't have time to play guessing games, Turner. What?"

"I almost had a real live Injun for Judge Ostwinkle to hang for horse stealin'."

"What? What happened?"

Turner launched into an account of how he had arrested an Indian or a half-breed, he wasn't just completely sure, and how the wily sonofabitch had broken away from Schuster, jumped the train, and escaped from the town.

"So?"

"So I been tellin' the people in town that he was one of them who held up the Centralia stage. That way, it'll all tie in with the story."

"Excellent. That was using your head, Turner."

A growl rumbled deep within the broad chest of the 'breed. The sheriff had deliberately tried to railroad him and have him hanged. Other Day was fully aware that no one in the town of Flea Hill would have believed him had he hung around for his trial. He paid closer attention when Jarting spoke again.

"What'd he look like, this Injun of yours?"

"Like an Injun. He had long hair, red headband, and a Stetson. You won't believe how he was armed. Big damn bowie knife in one boot, hunting knife in the other, and a throwin' knife down his back. Packed a .44 as well."

"And you let him get away?"

"I said Schuster did that."

There was an embarrassed silence, then Jarting spoke again. "Which way did he head out of Flea Hill?"

"On the eastbound. He must have jumped off sometime because Jake and me sure didn't find him on that there train. Damned near eleven miles. Sure was hard on our feet and all."

"If there's another shipment of money or gold we can stage another holdup and use his knives to let others think that he was involved."

"Can't."

"Why not?"

"Jake busted 'em."

"What the hell for?" Jarting demanded.

"Dunno. Somethin' to do, I guess."

"That man's stupid. When this is all over, I'll get rid of him," Jarting said.

A short silence followed and then Turner said, "Well, sir, I should get back to town. I'll be the better part of two hours gettin' there."

"Keep talking about this Injun who escaped. That way when we call the Army in, there'll be plenty of folks to back up the story."

"Yes, sir," Turner said.

Other Day heard Jarting stand and the door to the barn squeak open as they left.

What the hell had he heard? Some of it made sense but most of it didn't. It seemed to the half-breed that the two men were involved in some sort of shady deal that involved the Army and some Indians and holding up a stagecoach. But how it all tied together eluded him.

Other Day had planned on hanging around the Jarting ranch for a month, which would be long enough to put together a small stake to replace the money Turner had taken from him. He felt relieved that he had gotten away. From what he'd heard the crooked lawman say, Other Day could have been convicted of just about anything the sheriff would have wanted.

When he heard the sound of Turner's horse leaving, he went to the corral door and stepped outside. Scooping up a shovelful of manure, he heaved it into the wagon.

"You? Logan? Come here," Jarting yelled from the corral fence.

Other Day turned and studied the man as he slowly put the shovel against the wheel of the wagon. He walked toward the man and stopped when he was six feet or so from the rails of the fence.

"Yes, sir?"

"You rode in from the west the other day, didn't you?"

Other Day nodded.

"Did you see any renegade Indians out that way?"

Other Day shook his head.

"What'd you say your last job was?"

"I didn't."

"Well, what was it?" Jarting shifted impatiently from one foot to the other.

"I was a troubleshooter for a railroad up north."

Jarting slowly nodded. "I see. When you break the last horse in the remuda, you'll have to ride out and scout around for some wild mustangs to bring in. Be careful."

Other Day narrowed his eyes. "Yes, sir. I will."

Jarting turned and strode away.

Other Day watched him for a minute, then turned back to his job. What the hell had he stumbled into? He wasn't sure, but whatever it was, he'd have to be careful or he might wind up being one of the main actors in a play, the ending of which might not be to his liking.

CHAPTER SIX

Other Day walked slowly toward the chuckhouse. The dinner bell had run more than half an hour before, but he had wanted to finish with the mouse-colored gelding he'd been working with for most of the day. Once he'd ridden the horse and the animal had gotten all the bucking out of his system, the 'breed had waved a slicker in his face to get the newly broken mount used to things flapping around him. Then he had spent the last couple of hours mounting and dismounting, all the while talking to the gelding. The horse would be a good one, and since he had been the last one in the remuda, the herd of unbroken horses was gone and the remuda ready for restocking.

The half-breed's body ached from the jolting it had taken from the repeated shock of the horse landing on all fours after he had first mounted. The pain went with the job of breaking animals, but it had been too long a time since Other Day had done any such work. He'd drag his heels to delay a quick repeat of such punishment, but he'd help round up some likely looking horse flesh for the ranch if need be. Logan hoped that it would be near enough to payday and he would be able to leave with a few dollars in his pocket. He hitched up his pants and adjusted the rope belt he'd fashioned. That damned sheriff had managed to get everything of his from weapons to money. At least he'd managed to get the bay and his saddle, saddlebags, and Winchester.

He bent down to wash in the basin of water sitting on the low bench near the chuckhouse door. He could hear talking and laughter from inside while the other ranch hands ate their evening meal. After drying his hands and face, he went into the sodroofed log house.

A combination of smells greeted him and he threw a leg over the bench, next to a thick-muscled, tall man. He nodded his greeting and accepted a bowl of beans from the dark-complected man sitting across from him. Most of these men had just come in off the range.

"How'd it go today?" the last man asked.

Other Day looked up. "Good. I'm sore. But that goes with—"

"And you call yourself a bronc peeler?" the man sitting next to him asked.

"It's been a while," the 'breed said quietly.

"You must do some other type of work if you don't have to bust horses all the time for a livin'," the man sitting next to him said.

Other Day smiled grimly, thinking of the different jobs he'd had during his life. Instead of giving the gathered hands a rundown on his past, he simply said, "Yeah. I can do other things."

"Name's Bob Burgmeier," the man sitting across the table said. "Howdy."

Other Day nodded, acknowledging his introduction and said, "Logan's mine." When no one asked him about his first name, he relaxed a little. It was customary for most ranchhands to accept another's name as given. If he didn't want to tell them his first name, they would call him by the name he had offered.

One by one the men at the table introduced themselves, and when the one sitting to Other Day's right, mumbled, "Avery Longcamp," the 'breed nodded again.

The different plates of food were passed, and Other Day stocked up, satisfying his hunger. Venison and bacon along with boiled potatoes and sourdough bread were the evening's staples. When the cook, a small Irishman called Pancake, came in carrying a platter of hot biscuits to replenish the exhausted supply, Other Day took two. He dribbled molasses over the warm bread and dug in.

When he finished, he sat back and listened to the dinner table chatter as the men talked about different things that had happened that day.

When a lull filled the room, Avery Longcamp turned to the 'breed and said, "I still don't think much of a bronc peeler's takin' five dollars to bust a horse and comin' away hurtin'."

Other Day turned and stared at the man but said nothing.

"Yeah." Bob said from across the table. "You must be outta shape if you're hurtin' that bad. Whatcha been doin'?"

The 'breed studied Bob for a moment. Realizing the man's voiced carried no threat, unlike that of the man sitting next to him, he said, "I was up north, troubleshooting for a railroad that was being finished."

"I saw you ride in the other mornin'," Avery said. "I didn't see no six-gun on your hip."

Other Day turned to him again and said nothing. But his look carried the one word question, "So?"

"What I mean is," Avery said weakly, "you say you're a bronc-buster but you get stiff and sore from breakin' one horse. You say you been up north ridin' herd on trouble for some railroad or another. I think you're lyin', Mister, that's what I think."

"Best you change your mind right now, Mr. Longcamp," Other Day said softly, his voice carrying an unspoken threat to accompany the order.

"I suppose you're goin' to say next that you could change it for me if you wanted?"

Other Day looked across the table to Bob Burgmeier, then to the rest of them. "Is he always so trusting?"

"Yeah, what's wrong with you, Avery?" Bob asked.

"Ain't nothin' wrong with me. It's him. I think he's probably on the lookout for lawmen. What'd you do, anyhow, Logan?"

"I killed the whole crew on a ranch for thinking I was something I wasn't." Other Day stood and walked toward the door. Just as he reached it, whoops of laughter went up when the bulk of the men caught on to his answer. The last thing he heard before he stepped out into the cool evening air was Avery saying, "What you guys laughin' at, anyhow? He just owned up to bein' a killer."

Outside Other Day wondered when Jarting would send him out to scout up some new horses for the remuda. Another thing that he thought about was the lack of a foreman. He'd overheard one of the men say something about the head hand, John Henry Lutehoser, being out checking the herd of cattle. That meant the foreman would be returning soon. Perhaps when that happened, he'd be told to go out and look for horses, either wild ones or ones he could buy from some other ranch in the area.

Other Day walked around the ranch buildings to ease his sore muscles. It would be best if he did that rather than go to sleep right away. If he did the latter, he'd wake up in the morning and have to fight worse pain and stiffness simply to get out of his bed. When he reached the barn he heard the cookhouse door open and close. Without being obvious, he turned enough to see what was going on and watched as three men headed toward the bunkhouse.

Other Day didn't know if he'd ever want to sleep in there. The 'breed had bedded down with others outside since he'd arrived. The cell in which he'd been locked up, in Flea Hill, had been bad enough. But the bunkhouse at the Double J was downright awful as far as the 'breed was concerned. There had to be bugs inside, or the beds wouldn't have their legs sitting in cans of oil. Not that Other Day was bothered by bugs, but he didn't want to sleep with them. If the night was cool as the evening hinted it would be, a skunk or rattlesnake or some other varmint might get inside somehow. So, all in all, Logan decided he'd be better off outside.

A few minutes later, just as he was about to go around the last corner of the barn, the 'breed heard noise coming from the direction of the bunkhouse and turned to see the men coming outside with bedrolls.

On the side of the barn farthest away from the other buildings, Other Day stopped and looked out across the open expanse of land. He leaned against the wall and cleared his mind of the day's activities. He thought about Father David McGhee and the mission where he'd grown up. Was the priest still there? Was he still trying to teach other young boys and girls to read and write as he had Other Day? McGhee seemed to have a genuine love of his fellow man, but especially of the Indians with whom he worked.

Indians? The word registered in Other Day's mind and he replayed the conversation he'd accidentally overheard between Josiah Jarting and the sheriff from Flea Hill. That had been a close call, but as far as he knew, Turner might not have recognized him. The sheriff had seen him with his red headband and shoulder-length hair. Since he'd escaped from Flea Hill, the 'breed had cut his hair and stuffed the headband into his pocket. He thought back even farther and concluded that his name had not been mentioned, nor had the lawman or the judge even asked him what his name was, opting to address him as "Injun." If he shaved, no one in Flea Hill would know him.

He went back to the conversation he'd overheard that afternoon. That had to be something more than just a little peculiar. Jarting and the sheriff had spoken as if they knew a lot about the Centralia stage holdup. Was there some deep, dark reason that drove them to meet in the confines of Jarting's barn? From what he'd heard, Other Day concluded that Jarting had devised a plan to somehow run some Indians off their land, and once that was accomplished, Jarting intended to buy the land at a ridiculous price from the government to expand the size of his ranch. But the question that bothered Other Day was, how did Jarting plan to drive the Indians off the land? That would be no small accomplishment since the government would interfere if he tried. Jarting had to have some other way of doing it, but how? Why was the rancher running the risk of holding up stagecoaches to get the money to buy the land? That seemed at best a foolish move on his part.

Pushing away from the barn wall, Other Day walked back along the route he'd taken earlier. When he turned the corner, he could see in the gathering gloom of dusk the outlines of half-a-dozen men sleeping on the ground outside the bunkhouse. He was ready to join them.

Drawing near the sleeping men, Other Day moved without making a sound. He'd have to be quiet and lay for awhile until he got a stake together and would be able to move on. In the meantime, he'd keep his eyes and ears open to see if he could solve the puzzle he'd stumbled across.

The next afternoon, John Henry Lutehoser rode into the ranch. He pulled up his sorrel mare and dismounted. Other Day stepped out of the barn where he'd been straightening up the tack room.

"Who the hell are you?" Lutehoser asked.

"Name's Logan," Other Day said, concluding the man was the missing foreman.

"Where'd you come from? Who hired you?"

"Up north. Mr. Jarting and his daughter hired me to break horses. I'm out of work now that the last horse has been busted."

"We'll take care of that. The herd is north and west of here. 'Bout a hundred head. Day after tomorrow, you ride out and pick a dozen or so geldings to cut out. When you've done that, come back here and I'll send some hands out with you to bring 'em in."

"What'd they call you?"

"I'm John Henry Lutehoser, the forearm of the Double J. Just do your job and keep your nose clean and you'll get along real good here. Make trouble and you'll be sorry—real sorry."

Before Other Day could say anything, the foreman turned and strode away toward the ranch house. The 'breed followed him with narrowed eyes. Then a flash of color intercepted his attention and he focused on Mary Ann Hyburger, who came out of the ranch house and was walking toward the cookhouse. From what he could gather, the woman helped Pancake with his chores.

He frowned for a moment. He was positive that

there was something going on here at the Double J—something that was not completely open and aboveboard. It included not only the owner of the ranch, but the lawman from the neighboring town of Flea Hill.

He'd almost been sucked into playing a role in their scheme when he had been arrested in Flea Hill. Now one question rose above the others hammering at his brain. Was Mary Ann Hyburger, the stepdaughter of the owner, involved with Josiah Jarting's plan too?

He looked around the ranch buildings. Everything seemed natural and ordinary. Were the hired hands involved? Was he the only one ignorant as to what was going on? Or was he the only one who had stumbled onto the secret dealings of Josiah Jarting? Maybe his best bet would be to mount up, take his pay and get the hell out of there.

But his curiosity dominated his practical sense, and he turned to go back to the barn to continue his work in the tack room.

CHAPTER SEVEN

"Hey Shorty?" Other Day yelled to a cowhand passing by.

"What?"

"Come here and give me a hand for a minute." Other Day checked the lever he'd built under the rear axle of the wagon he was greasing.

"Whatcha need?" the man asked walking up to the 'breed.

"When I lift the rear of the wagon, put a block under the axle so I can take the wheels off and grease them."

Without a word, the short man walked over to the rear of the wagon and did as he was directed when the back end was raised.

"Thanks, Shorty," the 'breed said and went about his work.

"You'd better hope nobody gotta use that there

barn door you got blocked," Shorty said, pointing to the closed door.

Other Day looked at it. "I didn't put the wagon here in the first place. I was told to grease the axles and hubs and that's what I'm doing. I wasn't hired to pull wagons around. That's horses's work."

Shorty laughed and turned to go his way.

Other Day moved the grease pail to the rear of the wagon. After he removed the nut holding the wheel to the axle, he pulled the wheel off and leaned it against the box of the wagon. When he turned, he stopped short. Mary Ann Hyburger stood next to a table outside the cookhouse checking strips of beef jerky that were drying in the sun.

He stood for a long while admiring the woman. Her blonde hair shone brilliantly in the bright sunlight, and as if seeing her for the first time, Other Day took the opportunity to admire her. She was tall, a lot taller than most women he'd known, and large boned. But at the same time, despite her size, she moved with the grace and ease of a mountain lion stalking its prey. She didn't waste a motion. Each step, each movement of her hands and arms, appeared almost as if she'd planned them.

Other Day pictured her face in his mind. She was an attractive woman. More than attractive. She was downright beautiful. Her oval-shaped face was well balanced, and her blue eyes seemed as if they might be capable of fascinating any man who took enough time to look into them.

Other Day stood rooted to the spot, drinking in the view of Mary Ann, the mental picture of her face hovering in his mind. Then, little by little, the woman's hair darkened until it took on a strawberry-blonde hue. The smooth, creamy white complexion slowly changed to one dotted with a few freckles, and even the outline of the face altered until it was almost heart-shaped. The full lips curved into a broad, honest smile that teased and promised at thc same time.

The 'breed turned away. Belle Doolin! He had mentally changed Mary Ann's facial features to those of Belle Doolin. He shook his head and turned away. He had to stop thinking about the dead woman. It did no good. She was dead. He'd buried her. He'd killed the man responsible, choking him until his fingers had punctured the murderer's neck.

He closed his eyes and leaned his head against the wagon box. Clenching his fists, he wanted to beat on the unyielding wood to vent his frustration. He had loved Belle, but her memory was dominating his life. If he allowed it, her memory would consume him until it destroyed him.

He opened his eyes and caught sight of the grease pail standing near his feet. He didn't like the job he was doing, but it had to be done. He'd been told to do the lubricating by Lutehoser, the foreman, and he had best get going. It was the last set of wheels he had to grease. Crouching down, he picked up the loaded wooden paddle and smeared the grease on the axle end. Then with another glob, he stuffed the hole in the wheel hub. He dropped the paddle back into the pail and was about to position the wheel on the axle when he heard someone coming up behind him. His body suddenly bristled with the warning itch he experienced whenever a threat to himself was nearby.

He slowly turned and saw Avery Longcamp stop five feet away and glare, first at the wagon blocking the door to the barn, then at the 'breed. "What the hell you doin'?"

"Any dang fool can see what I'm doing," Other Day said softly. "I thought you worked on a ranch before."

"Don't get smart with me, you sonofabitch!" Longcamp took a step toward Other Day and stopped, his hands rolled into fists.

Other Day had heard from some of the others on the ranch that Longcamp thought of himself as a pretty good fighter and had whipped whoever he had fought. The only reason he took orders from Lutehoser and Jarting was because they saw to it that he was paid. Anyone else on the ranch, however, was fair game for his strong-arm tactics. Usually, to keep peace, the other men backed down from the bullying methods Longcamp used to get his way.

The last thing in the world Other Day wanted was a fight with this man who apparently wanted to fight for no reason that he could see. Greasing the wheels on a wagon was an annual job and had to be done. So what if the wagon did block the doorway to the barn. It wasn't the only way to get inside.

"There's one thing I don't allow, Mr. Longcamp," Other Day said quietly, "and that's someone insulting my mother. I think you'd better say you're sorry."

"What?" Longcamp stared at Other Day, a look of disbelief crossing his grizzled face. "I don't apologize to anybody—most especially a dumb sonofabitch like you!"

"You just did it again. Apologize. Now." The 'breed almost growled the last word, and he watched intently the face of the man confronting him. It had changed little as a result of the threatening manner in which Other Day had ordered him, but not as much as it should have. Other Day sensed the man would attack him any minute.

"Move the wagon and there'll be no trouble," Longcamp said.

"Why not go around to the side and go in that way if you have to do something so important in the barn?"

Longcamp shook his head and smiled derisively. "Because I want to use that there door you got blocked. Now, clear it or else."

Other Day stepped away from the wagon and stared at the man, his black eyes narrowing to slits. "Or else what?"

"Or else you're going to be damned sorry you didn't. I'll tear you apart."

"Sure, you will." Other Day took a step to his right, moving farther away from the wagon. It could be knocked off the pedestal Shorty had placed under the rear axle when Other Day had asked him. Somebody could be hurt seriously if the heavy vehicle was knocked off balance and fell.

"Look, Longcamp, I don't want to fight you. I have no quarrel with you. I'm just doing my job. Go around to the side and let's get on with our work." Other Day stopped moving, knowing that what he had just said would not dissuade the large men from doing what he wanted, which was to fight the half-breed.

"Afraid of me, huh? Heard what I've done to some of the other men when they crossed me, huh? Did they tell you what I done to three sons-a-bitches who got smart with me in the Thirsty Tonsil in Flea Hill?"

Other Day had only heard vague remarks about Longcamp's prowess as a fighter. He sized him up. He was about four inches taller than Other Day and outweighed him by 30 or 40 pounds. He was big and didn't seem to be afraid of the 'breed or anyone else.

"I don't think there's reason enough to fight, Longcamp. Go on about your business."

"You yellow sonofabitch!" Longcamp yelled and launched himself at the 'breed.

Other Day sidestepped the charge and turned to keep his eyes on his adversary like a bullfighter facing a bull.

Enraged because his initial offensive move had failed, Longcamp turned and glared at Other Day. "Stand still and fight like a man!"

Other Day kept his eyes on the man's belt buckle knowing that it would have to move when he did. All the feinting in the world with hands or feet were hollow gestures if the belt buckle didn't move. When it did, the whole man had to follow, and the 'breed would be ready when that happened.

Again, Longcamp tried to charge, but Other Day quickly leaped to the side, turning in midair to land on his feet, once more facing Longcamp. This time, Longcamp didn't go as far and stopped short, turning and lashing out with a balled up fist. It caught Other Day flush on the jaw and he felt his knees give a bit. The man's fists hit like a sledgehammer might feel.

A look of confidence crossed his face, as if he had the upper hand. Longcamp moved in for the kill when he saw Other Day's legs buckle for an instant. Rearing back, he launched another looping right hand.

This time, Other Day blocked it with his left arm and brought his own right around to the nose of Longcamp, hoping he'd draw blood. He felt the nose give, and warm blood splattered on his fist.

A roar of pain erupted from Longcamp's throat and he leaped forward, encircling Other Day around his upper body. The 'breed could not move his arms, and although he did his best to break the bearlike hug, he could not. Longcamp continued squeezing and Other Day could feel a peculiar light-headedness. He had to resist being beaten by such a hold. He stiffened his body and Longcamp suddenly stopped making headway bending the 'breed's back.

Still, the large man continued to exert pressure. Other Day could feel his head getting lighter and lighter, but he refused to allow the man to bend his back anymore.

After a few more minutes, Longcamp yelled, "Aw, shit!" and released the hold, lashing out with a ham-like fist to smash against Other Day's jaw.

The 'breed staggered backward, blood circulating without hinderance to his upper body, arms, and head. Almost giddy from the sensation, he managed to keep his eyes on the big man closing in on him for the finish of the fight.

Instead of striking him with his fists again, Longcamp threw both arms around the 'breed and began biting him on the neck and shoulders. Other Day screamed out in pain, shocked by the unexpected twist the man had given to the fight.

After he released his bite, Longcamp jumped to his feet and kicked at Other Day. The 'breed rolled over and over to get away from the huge booted feet, but Longcamp persisted and followed him, kicking and missing. Stopping unexpectedly, Other Day caught one of the feet as it came toward his head and twisted it hard. Longcamp went down in a heap.

Like a cat, Other Day leaped to his feet and found Longcamp doing the same. The two men eyed each other, then Longcamp charged again but was met by Other Day's fist on his broken nose. The large man went down and Other Day turned, keeping his attention full on his adversary.

Again, Longcamp got to his feet. Other Day wondered if the fight would go on forever and if Longcamp had ever lost a fight. Did he know how to lose?

Longcamp charged, but this time, Other Day caught the man's left hand and managed to avoid his swinging right fist. Pulling Longcamp toward his own body, Other Day clung tightly and fell back, bringing his knee up at the same time into Longcamp's crotch. Both men went down, Longcamp falling heavily across Other Day. He rolled off, scrambling to his feet. Other Day jumped to his own and swung with all his might.

The fist landed on Longcamp's jaw and the man

stopped moving, standing upright for an instant. His eyes glazed over, but he didn't fall. His right hand flew backward to strike out again, but before he could bring it forward, Other Day swung again. This time, Longcamp's right hand stayed put, frozen in midflight, and his eyes went more blank. Teetering for a long moment, he fell forward onto his face.

For the first time, Other Day became aware of some of the other ranch hands standing nearby watching the fight. He struggled to catch his breath and reached up to rub his bitten shoulder. Longcamp was a barroom fighter. Biting, scratching, kicking—anything went as long as it helped him win. This time he'd run into more than even he could handle.

Suddenly, Other Day flew forward, a sharp pain in the middle of his back. Something or someone had struck him from behind. It felt like two fists. He sprawled forward onto his belly and, when he rolled over, looked up into the angry face of John Henry Lutehoser.

"What the hell did you hit *me* for?" Other Day asked, sitting up. He reached for his throwing knife, then stayed his hand when he recalled that he no longer had it.

"I warned you, Logan. I told you to keep your nose clean but you didn't, and I told you if you didn't you'd get in trouble. Well, sir, you're in trouble."

Other Day slowly got to his feet. "I didn't start this fight. He—"

"You know it's funny, but I expected you to say something like that. By gadfrey, some of you drifters just amaze me. You know, if we didn't need horses broke, I'd fire you here and now."

"He didn't start the fight," Longcamp said from behind them.

Both Other Day and Lutehoser turned to face the beaten man.

"He didn't start it, I did."

"Ain't you ever gonna learn, Avery?" Lutehoser asked. "I told you to control your fighting, didn't I? Why the hell did you start it this time?"

Longcamp pulled himself to his feet and looked at Other Day. He shook his head and half-grinned. "I guess I wanted to see what he was made of, Mister Lutehoser. I was a little ornery this morning, and when I saw the barn door blocked, I thought I'd kick his ass."

"That ain't much of a reason." Lutehoser looked first at Longcamp, then at Other Day.

"I guess I had to show him I could beat him up like I done to nearly every other man-jack on the place, exceptin' you, of course, Mister Lutehoser."

"And you'd better not try it either. I got no time for ranch hands who do stupid things like this. Get back to work, Longcamp."

Avery Longcamp nodded and brushed his pants off.

"The rest of you *yahoos* get back to work," the foreman said, motioning with a sweep of his right arm toward the men who had witnessed the brawl. He turned back to the 'breed when they were alone. "As for you, Logan, you be outta here looking for that herd of horses before dawn tomorrow. Hear?"

Other Day nodded. "Do you want this wagon

anyplace in particular when I finish with it?"

"You can move it down by the small barn on the south side of the ranch. Just leave it there and somebody else'll put it away. Understand?"

The 'breed nodded and picked up the paddle in the grease bucket. He watched Lutehoser walk away.

After a short while, Longcamp came over to Other Day and extended his right hand. "Sorry 'bout gettin' you yelled at by the foreman. You're one helluva fighter, Logan."

Other Day studied him for a minute and realized he was seeing the real Avery Longcamp for the first time. The man was strong as an ox, but had a simplicity about him that suddenly appealed to the 'breed. Other Day usually felt that if a man apologized for something he'd done wrong it was a sign of weakness. When children did it, they were learning about life—learning what was right and what was wrong. He smiled enough to move the corners of his mouth. Avery Longcamp was still learning what was right and wrong in life. He took Longcamp's hand in a firm grip.

"I get feisty every now and then," the big man said, "and I gotta get it outta my system somehow. Fightin's a good way to get rid of it. You're a good fighter, Logan."

Other Day smiled broadly. "So are you."

Longcamp turned and walked around the corner of the barn toward the side door. Other Day shook his head. The man was like a big kid. In some ways, he reminded him of Theron Cullen. Both had childlike qualities, and Other Day wondered if he would become as close to Longcamp as he had to Theron. Maybe he should keep the big man at arm's length. It seemed to the 'breed that anyone he wound up liking usually met with a bad end. He'd have to wait and see. He went back to the wagon and moved the wheel into position to slide it onto the axle.

Later that night, after the evening meal, Other Day moseyed over toward Avery Longcamp's bedroll. The big man lay on his back apart from those who also chose to sleep under the stars.

"How're you feeling?" Other Day asked when he stood over him.

"Good. I mend fast. You?"

"A little stiff but nothing that's bothering me."

"That's good," Longcamp said.

"How long you worked for Jarting?"

"Almost a year now."

"I thought I saw a lawman around here a couple of days ago."

"You did. I guess old J.J.'s a friend of Turner's. He's from over at Flea Hill."

"He just comes out here to visit?"

"I reckon so. Why?"

"I don't know. Just wondering I guess." Other Day stopped for a moment. He didn't want to make Avery suspicious of anything. In time he might find something out from the big man.

"You got a nose problem?"

Other Day looked down at the man in the gloom of the darkening night. Maybe he wasn't as child-like as he first thought. "No. I don't think so. Why? You want to do something about it?"

Avery laughed. "Not with you. You're too good

a fighter. I'm the one with the nose trouble." He reached up and carefully wiggled it with one finger.

"How's it feel?"

"Awful. But I'll live. I've had it spread across my face more than once."

"I guess I hit you pretty hard."

"That you did. That you did. You ridin' out tomorrow mornin'?"

"Yeah. I'd better get to bed. Good night, Avery."

"Goodnight, Logan. Say, what's your other handle?"

"That's a big secret. Someday, I'll tell you."

Avery didn't answer and turned on his side. Other Day walked toward his bedroll, noting the dark shapes of the buildings in the gloom of the night. When he looked toward the south, he stopped short and focused his eyes. Where was the wagon? He could see the small barn to which he had taken the wagon with the help of several of the other hands. He could see the outline of the building, but the box wagon, which had been left in front of the west side were the door was, was gone. What difference did that make? Probably Lutehoser had done what he said he'd do and had somebody else put it away.

By the time Other Day lay down in his own bedroll, Avery's snoring rumbled through the night like distant thunder. The 'breed stretched and propped his hands behind his head for a moment and looked at the stars. Then he closed his eyes and went to sleep.

CHAPTER EIGHT

The 'breed had been away from the Double J for the last day and a half. He'd found the herd of horses late afternoon the day before. After observing them most of the morning of the second day, he had considered his options and decided to return in a day or so to cut out a dozen animals for the remuda at the ranch. As far as he knew, he'd be paid five dollars a head for each one he broke. That would mean $65, including the other bronco he'd already gentled. That money, coupled with the $30 he'd pick up for a month's work as a ranch hand, would give him enough of a stake to get out and away from the domain of Josiah Jarting.

Other Day reined up and patted the neck of the mouse-colored gelding he had broken. The time he had spent with the animal had been wisely invested. The horse would prove to be an invaluable mount to the Double J once his training was complete. Right then it seemed the only one who could ride the gelding was Other Day. The animal tended to shy away from the other hands when they approached. But he did tolerate the 'breed and didn't show any of the rabbity signs he did when other ranch hands were about.

Logan mumbled some of the Comanche "trade" language he knew from the time he had spent with that people, learning their ways with horses. His voice caressed the words smoothly, the rolling r's working their peculiar effect on the animal.

Other Day frowned when the thought of Jarting came again. There was something about him that bothered Other Day. The secret meeting Jarting'd had with the sheriff seemed to confirm in the 'breed's mind that there was something a little crooked about the man.

His mount dropped his head to crop some grass from the hill and the 'breed let go of the reins for a moment. A brisk wind blew up and he turned to check the sky. Clouds, which had been building on the western horizon all morning, were moving toward him. It would rain within a short time. He could smell it on the wind. He clucked to the horse and he jerked his head up for an instant, then shook it and moved out. Riding the horse in a normal manner would put him back at the ranch in three to four hours.

After crossing a ridge, he reined up short. The wreckage of an overturned buckboard lying in an arroyo below him arrested his attention. Turning the gelding so he would head in that direction,

Other Day kept his eye on the broken vehicle. When he climbed down from the saddle, he walked over to it, keeping the reins in his hands. The small wagon looked unweathered. The appearance of the wagon led the 'breed to conclude that it had not been in the gully very long. Closer examination showed the half-breed that the doubletree and tongue were gone. The team pulling it had runaway with it and gotten completely away when they had somehow become separated from the buckboard itself.

Logan wondered what had happened to the driver and if the wagon belonged to the Double J. He had noticed a similar vehicle at the ranch, but had not looked at it closely enough to remember if it was now lying in the ditch below him.

After remounting, he rode through the arroyo and began following the wheel marks. Within several hundred yards, he found the tongue. From the length of it and the broken end, Logan could tell that it had snapped off somehow. Then he noticed that there weren't any wheel marks about. He turned in the saddle and saw where they were behind him, then rode forward in a slow deliberate way until he came to a couple of boulders that jutted up from the floor of the hillside. Just beyond, he saw the wheel marks again and scratched his head. There weren't any hoofprints from the team all along the way, which meant that they had become separated from the buckboard farther back. The tongue must have jammed against the boulders and thrown the wagon into the air, snapping off the tongue at the same time. The buckboard then must have continued on its wheels once it landed and finally stopped in the arroyo. The pin holding the doubletree to the tongue had become dislodged and the team had run away from the buckboard when the singletree at the point of the tongue loosened.

Other Day pushed the gelding into a trot and rode up the hill. When they reached the crest, the 'breed pulled up and walked the horse forward until he could see across into the next valley. When he could, he froze in the saddle for an instant, then leaped from the animal's back, grabbing the Winchester as he did. Dropping the reins of the gelding to the ground, he hoped the animal wouldn't stray too far or run off once he realized his rider was not paying any attention to him.

Other Day threw himself to his belly and crawled until he could see into the valley, but would not show himself in a prominent way at the same time. He eyed two forms lying ahead of him. One was a woman wearing a blue and white dress. The form that concerned him was behind the woman, but creeping toward her: it was an Indian. The half-breed had gathered from listening to different bits and pieces of conversation during meals and after work in the evenings that there wasn't another ranch within 15 miles to the south or 12 miles to the north, and Flea Hill lay to the east. Logan had ridden west since leaving the ranch the day before, and there was supposed be be nothing in that direction for miles except an Indian reservation someplace in Colorado. It was a Ute reservation according to what one of the cowhands had said.

Narrowing his eyes, Other Day cocked the

Winchester and sighted along the barrel. The Ute was perhaps only 20 feet away from Mary Ann. Even from a distance, Logan recognized her. And though he wanted to rescue her, he couldn't run the risk of trying to hit the Indian because he might hit Mary Ann. It would be best to shoot to the right of the Ute's head and hope that the sound of the rifle and the knowledgc that there was someone around to help the stricken woman would scare him off.

Slowly squeezing the trigger, Other Day aimed to the right and high. The crack of the Winchester rang out and echoed off the low hills. The Indian, who had been a mere ten feet away from Mary Ann, stood upright and turned, running toward a stand of scrub trees. In seconds, he was mounted and riding as fast as he could toward the hills in the south.

Other Day stood and turned to find the mouse-colored gelding bucking 100 yards away. The rifle shot had scared him. Logan hoped he could get close enough to talk to the animal. Without appearing to hurry, he moved as quickly as he could and the animal turned to watch him approach. When he was within earshot, Other Day began talking, using the Comanche trade language. The horse cocked his ears forward and remained still. Other Day patted his neck when he had grabbed the reins and swung into the saddle. The gelding danced a bit and then responded to his rider's commands. He quickly rode to the still figure.

Other Day looked for something to which he could tie the horse and found a small boulder. He tipped it up to put the leather straps beneath, then hurried over to Mary Ann. He could see no wound or blood, and when she moaned after he turned her onto her back, he relaxed. In seconds she fluttered her eye lids and opened them.

"Where—What happened? Who are you?" she asked fixing her attention on the figure hovering over her.

"Take it easy, Miss Hyburger. You're all right. You lost your buckboard and got knocked out when you were thrown. How do you feel?"

"Just who are you?" she demanded and sat up. When she recognized him, she said, "Logan? Thank God you found me. I might have died out here alone. I have no weapon and I'm sure no one at the ranch would have thought to look in this direction when they began searching for me."

"Why's that? Some of those men could sure have tracked your buckboard."

"I had started out heading toward the south. I was just going for a ride and I wanted something different. Well, I sure got it." She stopped and looked at him for a moment. "I thought I heard a shot from way off in the distance. Did I?"

He nodded. "A Ute was stalking you. I shot my rifle to scare him off. It worked."

"A Ute? What would a Ute be doing this close to the ranch?"

"He looked too short to be anything else. The Snake Nation's to the north and this is too far south and east for them. So it wasn't a Shoshoni. And we're too far east for Paiute. So the only Indians left are Utes. What happened to you?

Something scare your team?"

She nodded. "A rattlesnake spooked them. I almost had them under control when the front wheel hit a rock or something and I was thrown out."

"That's what I figured happened. The buckboard is shot. We'll have to ride double to get back to the ranch. I hope it don't skitter my horse." He motioned with his head toward the gelding. "We'd better get going before it rains. Maybe we can get back without it—" He stopped when the first drops struck. The wind picked up and he looked around. Spotting the grove where the Ute had hidden his horse, he said, "Can you make it to that grove?"

She clambered to her feet in way of answer and started toward it. Other Day picked up the reins of the gelding and led him toward the trees. The wind continued blowing and the rain increased, pelting them unil they reached the protection the trees offered.

The rainfall lessened considerably once they were beneath the branches. After tying the gelding to one of the tree trunks, Logan quickly gathered some of the fallen branches and built a small fire to help keep Mary Ann and himself warm and dry. The rain fell on the flames, but not sufficiently to put it out.

They sat down and said nothing for several minutes. Mary Ann broke the quiet.

"Your name is Logan—right?"

He nodded.

"What's your first name?"

He glanced over at her. She was not hard to look

at, and he wouldn't have minded telling her his name, sharing the rather humorous story of the mix-up that happened the day he was baptized. But if he told her his right first name, the chances of his half-breed heritage being known by others and the possibility of the sheriff finding out that a half-breed was working at the Double J might lead to his being discovered and taken back to Flea Hill for trial. He had done nothing wrong and would protect himself no matter what. He couldn't trust Mary Ann Hyburger with that information.

He smiled crookedly and said, "Logan's enough. I'll answer to that."

"How are you feeling?" she asked.

His head jerked up. "Feeling? What do you mean?"

"Aren't you stiff and sore from the fight with Avery Longcamp?"

"No." He had hurt some when he mounted the mouse-colored gelding the morning before, but he felt fine right then.

They fell silent for several minutes, then Other Day thought of the sheriff's visit to the ranch. After bringing up the subject, he finished by asking, "Is that a common thing?"

"Ivo rides out every now and then. He and Josiah are pretty tight, I reckon."

"What about the different names you two got?"

"Oh, that. Well, he married my mother when I was small. She died about four years ago, when I was fourteen. He just sort of took over the ranch from what I know."

"You mean it was your mother's ranch?"

"My folks'. My Pa died when I was less than a year old. He'd started the ranch a few years before. Ma couldn't make it go, and when Josiah asked her to marry him, she did with the hope of saving the ranch. It worked but it's more Josiah's now than it ever was my folks or mine. He's built it up and—" Mary Ann broke off, then said, "Say? Why am I telling you everything when you won't even tell me your first name?"

He shrugged and forced a smile. "I got my reasons."

"You on the run from the law?"

"Not really. I've done nothing wrong."

"Then, why not tell me your first name?"

"I will someday, maybe."

Again they fell silent, and the only sound in the grove was the pattering of rain drops on the trees as the rain filtered down to splash gently about.

Other Day reflected on the conversation he'd just had with Mary Ann. The way she had told him things suggested to him that if her stepfather was involved in something shadowy she didn't know about it. It was either that or she was the slickest liar Other Day had ever run into.

"You know something about Indian land to the west of the ranch?" he asked.

She frowned and said, "There's a Ute reservation southwest of here. Why?"

He shrugged. "Are they friendly? Do they ever come close to the ranch like that Ute buck I chased?"

"I don't think so. If staying on their land and not

coming around makes them friendly, then I guess they're friendly. We seldom see them."

"And still, one of the Utes was stalking you."

"Maybe he was going to try to help me."

"That might be."

"You shot at him to scare him off." She studied the 'breed for a long time, then leaned forward as if to look at him even more closely. "Are you part Indian?"

Other Day leaned back in a defensive move. "Me? Why?"

"You're dark enough to be one. You don't wear anything that looks like what an Indian should wear, but you're dark. You sure about that?"

He grinned weakly. "I should know, shouldn't I?" Other Day felt uncomfortable not telling the whole truth. It was the first time he had ever avoided telling of his heritage. Most of the time he felt proud of his heritage, not because of the Indian blood, but because of his mother. She had been so smart and intelligent and beautiful until Half-Ear Hantlemann got finished with her. He shuddered and looked away, hoping Mary Ann hadn't noticed the sudden change. For some reason, he wanted no one at the ranch to know of his background. Why jeopardize his freedom? He had done nothing wrong.

"I guess," he said, turning back to look at the woman, "I'm just dark. My mother and father were both dark like me."

"I see."

Other Day looked at her. She was a large woman, but not fat or clumsy looking. She had a certain instinctive grace that was almost animal-like in the way she moved and walked.

"Say, Miss Hyburger, are there any plans for Josiah to expand the ranch that you know about?"

She puckered her lips and shook her head. "Not that I know of. It's pretty much hemmed in on three sides, and to the west is the Indian reservation."

A thick silence fell over the grove once more during which Other Day stood. It had stopped raining. "I think we'd best get going. It'll be dark before we get home."

She got to her feet and followed him out of the clearing. The gelding shied away from Logan when he went to mount. But after a moment, he was able to swing into the saddle without trouble. The gelding sidestepped when he pulled Mary Ann onto the horse behind him. She hung on tightly for fear of slipping off the bedroll and saddlebags on which she sat sidesaddle.

Several hours later, the gelding walked into the ranch yard and the men, who had been gathered around the chuckhouse, waved or made known their welcome back, then broke up, heading for the bunkhouse.

"You sonofabitch!" Josiah Jarting yelled from near the chuckhouse. "What the hell are you doing with her?" He leaped from the wagon and stalked toward the 'breed, who had pulled up on the gelding and helped Mary Ann get off.

Other Day dismounted and stared at Jarting who stormed up. One of the other ranch hands took the reins of the gelding and led him away.

"Answer me right now!" He turned his attention from the 'breed to Mary Ann. "Are you all right? Did he hurt you?"

"Hurt me? He saved my life. Why are you yelling? I thought you'd be happy to see me."

"Well, I am. What happened? How'd he save your life?"

She told him what had happened and how Other Day had scared the Ute off. Jarting blanched when he heard the story and mumbled an apology to Other Day, who merely nodded, and made a mental note of the man's reaction to the part about the Indian being chased away.

"Did you find the herd of horses?"

Other Day nodded. "I've got twelve or so spotted. I'll take a few men back tomorrow and cut them out."

"No, you won't," John Henry Lutehoser said from behind the 'breed.

Other Day turned. "Why not?"

"Tomorrow's payday and the men will be headin' for Flea Hill. When they get back, you can go after the broncs."

Other Day nodded. He turned to leave. "Good night, Miss Mary Ann. Good night, Mr. Jarting. John Henry."

The two men grunted and turned to walk away, Jarting heading for the house with his daughter and John Henry for the bunkhouse.

"Good night, Logan, and thank you," Mary Ann said over her shoulder.

Other Day nodded and walked to the bunkhouse. He took his bedroll from in there and spread it on the ground outside. The air was clean and clear after the rain. He would sleep well.

Once he lay on his back apart from the others who were sleeping outside, he stared at the stars. Why had Josiah Jarting reacted so strangely at the mention of the Indian he'd scared?

CHAPTER NINE

Other Day scrubbed his hands and dried them on the long roller towel hanging from the side of the bunkhouse. He looked in the mirror and shook his head. His beard needed shaving off, and his hair was still disheveled from the hurried cutting he'd given it before riding into the Double J.

The sound of the other ranch hands laughing filled the air. It was payday and they were going to Flea Hill.

Other Day turned away from the mirror and walked toward the entrance of the bunkhouse. There'd be no celebrating in town for him, not in Flea Hill. It would be just his luck to have the sheriff or his greedy deputy recognize him and throw him back into jail. Logan's appearance had changed with the haircut and without the Stetson and red headband that his mother had made for him so long ago. The likelihood that the sheriff or deputy would recognize him seemed remote, but he wouldn't take a chance with his freedom as long as he held doubts.

Some of the men inside were putting on clean clothes, while others didn't think it necessary, choosing instead to go to town wearing the same wool pants and shirt they had for the last month.

Other Day plopped down on the bunk he was supposed to use at night.

Avery Longcamp walked over. "Will you get goin'? We gotta lotta livin' to do tonight."

"You'll have to count me out, Avery."

"What? You gotta go! It's your right to go into town and blow off some steam. Why there's the cutest little angel at the Thirsty Tonsil. Name's Suellen. Why she'd have you grinnin' from ear to ear like a mountain lion in a slaughterhouse before you knew what was happenin'."

Other Day winced at the name. He knew Suellen. She'd tried her womanly best to bed him. There was also the distinct possibility she might recognize him even if the sheriff and the deputy did not. "No, I don't think so, Avery. Thanks just the same."

"Hell's fire, don't thank me, boy. I ain't talked you into it. I sure don't see how you can want to hang around this here dog house or go outside to that flea trap of a bedroll of yours when you could go into town and get a nice shave and sit in a hot tub before goin' to see one of them there fallen angels. No sir! What the hell is this country comin' to, anyhow?"

Before Other Day could answer, Josiah Jarting

entered and sat down at one of the two tables. The men automatically quieted and lined up for their pay. Other Day knew he only had a few days pay coming and perhaps five bucks for breaking the mouse-colored gelding. Even if he wanted to go into town with the boys, he wouldn't be able to afford much fun. He smiled to himself. Even if he still had the money Turner had taken from him, he wouldn't go in just to have fun. That wasn't his style.

When his name was called out, Other Day stepped to the table and took his money. When he counted it, he found $11. Without comment, he put it in his pants pocket and went back to his bunk. Jarting must have paid him five dollars for the gelding. Logan hadn't expected more than six or seven dollars for the few days he'd been employed.

"All right, men, you have your money. I'll be heading for Flea Hill within the next fifteen minutes. If you want to ride with me, be saddled up and ready to go."

Most of the cowhands followed within seconds, but Avery stopped at the door. "Sure you won't come along?"

Other Day looked up. "If I do, I'll look you up when I get there."

"Just follow the road east of here. It'll take you right into Flea Hill."

When he was alone, Other Day walked outside and watched as the men rode away. He stepped to the mirror again. If his hair was smoothed out a little and he shaved, he'd look nothing like he had when he'd been in Flea Hill. He went back inside and borrowed Avery's straight-edge razor. While he lathered his face, he thought about the fact that he had to shave. He'd known a few half-breed men in his time, and most of them hadn't had to shave very much. After he finished, he stepped back from the mirror.

"Well, now, ain't yuh purty," Pancake, the cook, said stepping around the corner of the bunkhouse.

Other Day turned to find him smiling, showing the gaps where teeth had been knocked out for some bad cooking job or other. "No, I'm not pretty. What I need is a decent haircut. Is there a good barber in Flea Hill?"

"There's a good one right here. I'll fix you up. Your hair looks like you chewed it off somehow. Come on over to the chuckhouse and I'll lower yer ears for yuh."

Twenty minutes later, Other Day felt his own mother, had she been alive, would have had trouble recognizing him. After borrowing a clean shirt and pants from Avery's store of possessions, he went to the corral and saddled a dun mare and mounted. Waving to Pancake, he rode out of the ranch yard. He caught a flurry of color out of the corner of his eye and saw Mary Ann Hyburger go into the ranch house. The bay gelding might give him away if Schuster, the deputy, really had his heart set on owning the animal and recognized him. But since the mouse-colored gelding was too rabbity to take to town, he had opted for the mare.

When he reached the road Avery had mentioned, he turned eastward and rode the mare at a good trot toward Flea Hill. Two hours later, he walked the mare into town. Other Day couldn't believe his eyes. The place was thriving with activity. It was nothing like the dead, sleepy little town he'd ridden into eleven days earlier. There must have been hands from other ranches and ranch people in town to stock up on supplies for the month. He wondered why Pancake hadn't come into town.

Still, the idea that he was even there bothered Other Day. He was running one big risk in being there. All it would take was one of the three people who had seen him there before to notice him. Nevertheless, he was curious about some of the conversation he'd overheard in the barn and wanted to see if he might pick up something along those lines in town. It would be tight for him until he was absorbed by the crowd which he was sure had gathered at the Thirsty Tonsil.

He angled the mare toward the saloon and tied her up along with the other 20 ponies already there. He opened the door of the barroom and stepped inside. A fiddle and banjo were being played, and some of the whores were dancing with ranch hands who hadn't seen a woman for 30 days or more. Logan made his way to the bar and ordered a beer.

A hand clapped him on the back and he turned, ready for anything but feeling naked without his weapons. He hadn't brought the Winchester in for fear it would stir up trouble of some sort. Tonight, he had to be as passive as he had ever been in his life.

"Well, now if it ain't my old fightin' partner, Logan." Avery Longcamp smiled in a silly way and leaned foward on the bar.

"You're feeling pretty good already, aren't you?" Other Day looked him over and then faced the bar again.

"Oh, yeah, I am. It don' take much to make me the happiest cowpoke in the whole world. You know?"

"That's good." Other Day picked up the beer when the bartender placed it in front of him. The man turned away and Other Day felt he'd passed the first, albeit the weakest, test when the bartender who had faced him that first day left without saying anything at all.

"Say, Logan, my friend, I'm buyin' you the next one. We'll make it whiskey and a beer. And—" He stopped and reached out to finger the shirt Other Day wore. "That sure looks familiar. I got one just like it."

"I hope you don't mind. I borrowed yours. You made coming to town sound like the thing to do, that I just had to follow."

"That's fine. You can wear it. Wanna fight?"

"Not tonight. Besides, we've already fought. Remember?"

"Oh, yeah, we did, didn't we." Avery stared at the 'breed and worked on focusing his eyes. "Say, looky there! How's about tellin' me about the scars on your face there. How'd you get them?"

Other Day didn't want to tell him the story. It dredged up too many bad memories of his mother's death and how he had been pistol-whipped by Half-Ear Hantelmann when he had tried to save her. He forced a crooked smile. "It was one helluva fight."

Avery turned back to the bar and lifted his shot glass. The man was drunk, but there was something about him now that appealed to the 'breed.

He thought he might be able to trust this man, drunk or sober. He fought well and he was honest. He had owned up to the fact that he, not Other Day, had started the fight when Lutehoser struck the 'breed from behind. That meant he had some sort of principles in his life. He made a mental note to learn more about Avery Longcamp when the man was sober.

Just then, the door opened and a hush fell over the room. The 'breed turned to see who had come in and turned back immediately when he saw Ivo Turner and Jake Schuster standing near the door. They were in either to look over the crowd or to arrest somebody. Other Day suddenly realized he was the only one with his back to them. Turning slowly, he picked up his beer and raised it to his lips. He watched over the rim of his mug as the two lawmen wound their way through the crowded saloon. They passed within two feet of him and didn't pay him the least bit of attention. Turner nodded to someone in the corner, and Other Day looked in that direction after the lawmen had passed. Josiah Jarting sat alone at a corner table, sipping from a glass of whiskey. The nod from the sheriff had been so slight that Other Day would have missed it if it hadn't happened directly in front of him.

The 'breed took another sip of beer and watched Turner and Schuster leave. Within seconds, Jarting threw down the rest of his drink and stood. Picking up the bottle, he made his way toward the door.

The bartender came to the end of the bar where Other Day stood and said, "Mr. Jarting said he wanted to buy his boys a drink when he left. Who's with the Double J?"

A clamor of voices sounded and the drinks were poured. Other Day picked up his fresh beer and sucked at the foam. Was Jarting going to meet the sheriff? If he was, what was going on between them? Were they going someplace where the 'breed might be able to overhear them? The only way he could find out was to follow the owner of the Double J.

"I'll see you a little later, Avery," Other Day said and left the bar. He wasn't sure if Avery had heard him and didn't see that it mattered whether he had or hadn't. Where the 'breed was going was his business and no one else's.

Halfway across the room, Other Day felt a hand on his arm, and he turned to look into the face of Suellen, the whore.

"Hey, Handsome, you ain't leavin', are you?"

"I've got some business to tend to." Other Day pulled himself free of the woman's grasp and moved toward the door.

"You know, you and me could probably have the best party of the night at my place if you wanted to go there with me." She grabbed him again.

"I said I have business." He saw her looking at him closely and wondered if she recognized him.

"Oh, come on, Handsome. Don't leave. You make this place a little more tolerable."

Other Day continued moving toward the door when she threw both arms around him. He turned to face her and she reached for his crotch. He quickly sidestepped the motion and hurried toward the exit, hoping she wouldn't be able to identify him. He had heard of a harlot in the New

Mexico Territory who could tell, when she wore a blindfold, who was in bed with her just by touching and feeling her bed partner. He couldn't run the risk that Suellen had a similar ability.

When Other Day reached the boardwalk on the outside of the Thirsty Tonsil, he stopped and looked up and down the dark street. At first, he saw nothing. Then a shaft of light from across the street caught his attention, and he saw Josiah Jarting entering the courthouse. When the door closed, the street was dark once more.

Other Day moved off to his left, toward the railroad depot. He'd come up from behind the courthouse along the tracks, since he figured that approach would considerably reduce the chances of his being seen.

He made no effort to cover the sound of his footsteps until he reached the west side of the station. Then, he moved like a ghost as he headed toward the tracks. He followed them in the direction of the courthouse, and when he stood at the back of it, he went to the side where the sheriff's office was. There, he made his way toward the glow of a burning coal-oil lamp that sat in the window.

The night was warm enough that the window would be open. Logan silently made his way toward it and smiled grimly when he began hearing voices.

Keeping the light between him and the street and standing well back in the shadows would assure him that no one from the street side would see him. He pressed against the wall and listened.

"Well," Ivo Turner said, "here's to your plan. I hope it works the way you say it will."

"Don't worry about that, my friend. It'll work,"

Jarting said confidently.

A clink of glasses sounded and was followed by a moment of silence as the men downed their drinks.

"I assume," Jarting said, "that you're not letting the people forget that the Indians are responsible for the mayhem that's going on."

"Whether there is any or not. I've been keepin' them thinkin' about that Injun who got away from Jake. Hell, if we brought in any Injun right now, the jury'd find him guilty as all get out for the Centralia stage holdup. Wouldn't have to be the one we had. Any redskin'd do!"

"That's fine. I assume then that you have no idea as to where the one who got away might be?"

"Nope. I'll say this, he's as sneaky as any Injun I ever run into."

"How do you mean?"

"He come back and got his horse in the dead of the night and nobody heard 'im when he skedaddled. The deputy wanted that horse, too."

"Well, just keep reminding them townspeople who was responsible."

"We haven't stopped talking about him. You shoulda seen the knives and such we took off him. He even claimed he was a half-breed one time. It woulda been better if we coulda had a trial. That would make everyone remember better."

"Maybe it's a good thing that he did get away," Jarting said.

"How do you figure?"

"Well, this way you can keep asking people if they've seen him. A trial could be forgotten shortly after it was over. By the way, what was his name?"

"Don't know. Never did find out. Neither did Judge Ostwinkle."

"What's he look like, in case I should run across him?"

"Like an Injun that tries to be a white man. Dressed in regular clothes but with long hair. He wore a red headband and a Stetson that's still here. Packed a .44 Colt. That's over there on the wall. He was pretty light for a redskin. He mighta been a half-breed. I don't know."

"Well, that don't sound like him."

'Whatcha mean, Mister Jarting? Who're you talkin' about? Sound like who?" Turner asked, then added, "Pour you 'nother?"

"Sure. I was thinking of a man I just hired a while back at the ranch."

"What about him?"

A short silence followed and then Turner said, "Here's lookin' at you."

Other Day could hear the glasses being put back on the desk or table. Perhaps he'd been too hasty to come to town. What if Jarting sought him out and wanted to show him to the sheriff? That could be a real test of his changed appearance. His best bet was to get out of town or stay out of sight until the Double J people left town and then follow them back to the ranch. When Jarting cleared his throat, Other Day leaned a bit closer to make sure he heard everything.

"Nothing much. He's dark but he doesn't answer the rest of your description. More than likely he's just what he claims to be. A drifter in from the north."

"What's his handle?"

"Logan."

"Logan? What's his first name?" Turner suddenly sounded excited.

A long pause followed. Then Jarting said, "You know, I don't know. I think he never did tell us or maybe he just refused to tell us. Come to think of it he said he'd answer to Logan, said that that was good enough."

"Lord, I hope it ain't Other Day Logan."

"Who?"

"Other Day Logan. Ever hear of him?" Turner asked, a peculiar note in his voice.

"No. Who is he?"

"Let me tell you what I know about that sonofabitch!"Turner said, dropping his voice somewhat.

Other Day leaned even closer to make sure he didn't miss anything the sheriff said.

CHAPTER TEN

"You ever been to Bell's Town?" Turner asked.

"No. I know where it is, but I've never been there." Jarting said.

"Well, sir, this Other Day Logan must be a crazy man. He took on the sheriff and the guy that owned the town. Seems they had pushed Logan around a little or somethin' and he thought the sheriff had killed his girl friend or somethin' like that. Anyhow, he wound up killing some fifteen or twenty men who worked for Ace Hanlon, the town big shot. He used his bare hands to damn near tear the sheriff's head off. Can you imagine that?"

"Who told you this?" Jarting asked.

Other Day shook his head. He knew he hadn't killed that many men. He had taken on some three or four deputies and wound up shooting them or stabbing them with one of his knives. He had slain

Ace Hanlon with a bowie knife in the throat that had almost beheaded the man. Logan thought back for a moment to the instant he realized his thumbs had punctured Ike Furlong's throat. The townspeople had had to pull Other Day off the murderer.

"Man named Teaheart. A drummer who had passed through Bell's Town shortly after everything quieted down. He just missed the fight, I guess."

Jarting coughed and said, "Pour me one more."

After a few minutes of silence during which the two men drank again, the ranch owner said, "You said he killed quite a few men. Do you know what weapons he used?"

"Come to think of it, Teaheart said something about a six-gun and some knives. Why?"

"Your Injun had some knives, remember?"

"Bar the door, Nelly. I never once thought of that. Do you suppose he coulda been that wild man?"

"Damned if I know."

A short pause followed and then Turner said, "Naw. I don't think so. That Injun mighta been armed to the teeth but he wasn't a fighter. Hell's fire, he ran like a scared rabbit to get away. He's like all Injuns—scared of his own shadow and rabbity as a worthless horse. Naw, he's not the same man."

Other Day narrowed his eyes and a low, rumbling growl broke from his chest. He quieted down when Turner continued.

"I'll tell you one thing though, Mister Jarting, you'd better be careful of that new hand you got workin' for you. If he's the same Logan I heard tell about, you'd best fire him and send him on his way. He sure sounds like a dangerous trouble-maker to me. Shoot! I'd get rid of him if I was you."

"Tell me, Sheriff, what you'll do if it turns out that he's the one who got away from you?"

"Why, shoot the sonofabitch, of course. He's a danged fugitive. Ain't no reward on him but that doesn't make any difference. He's a wanted man." Turner laughed and was joined by Jarting.

Other Day scowled. He'd have to be on his guard for a while to see what Jarting would do in way of trying to trick him into divulging his full name.

"Gettin' back to your plan, Mister Jarting, you about ready to move ahead?"

"Yes, sir. I've bought and cached guns and ammunition at the ranch for the Utes on the reservation. A lot of whiskey, too. When they get drunk on hooch, they'll start listening to anything anybody says. I intend to have Little Eyes egg them on and get all of them the hell off the reservation to do some hunting and raiding and to try driving the white men off their land."

"What if he can't do that?"

"Don't worry, he can. He's gaining power with the younger bucks every day. I'll tell him what I want to do to get him upset and he'll pass it on. The rest of those worthless savages will follow him, especially after they start downing that cheap liquor. Once they leave the reservation and start causing trouble, it'll be your responsibility as sheriff to send for the Army to help you put them back on the reservation."

"Where're the redskins now?"

"On the reservation. I set up meetings with Little Eyes by smoke at high noon whenever we gotta talk. We meet at Twin Springs."

"What if they attack your place when they got their hooch and rifles?"

"They won't. But if they do, they'll only take any suspicion off me. Oh, there's going to be blood spilled. I know that. When that happens, I'll get the ranchers together and demand that you get the Army here pronto. Somebody, me if no one else suggests it, will tell the Army that these Utes should be moved farther west. Then I'll buy up their reservation from the government real cheap and double the size of my ranch."

"Sure seems like a passel of trouble to get some land. Why not just buy out the ranches on the north or south of your place?"

"I asked them but they won't sell. Besides, I'm doing the community a real favor by getting rid of the Injuns, ain't I?"

Other Day growled and fought the urge to dive through the window to mete out his style of justice. Jarting was a real troublemaker and should be stopped. The bastard was going to take advantage of the dumb drunk Indians again. Was it any wonder he hated both as much as he did? He wished he could do something about his heritage and take sides with one or the other. It was hell being caught in the middle as he was. His hand dropped to his hip and he stopped. His .44 was not there. Other than the Winchester, he was weaponless.

"Of course you'd be doin' all of us a favor,

Mister Jarting."

Another silence followed, then chairs scrapping on the wood floor sounded, and Other Day leaned away from the window, pressing against the wall.

He could hear the men saying something as they left the office, but couldn't make it out. When he heard the door open and close, he waited a few minutes and stepped to the window. Both men had gone. He leaned in and could see his Colt and holster hanging from a peg behind the desk.

Without thinking anymore about it, he threw a leg over the sill and pulled himself inside. He moved quickly to the wall and took the gun. Hanging from the peg beneath the gun belt, he found his pants belt and took it as well.

He slipped out of the office and back into the shadows. He had to hide the gun and belt someplace. He'd been seen in the Thirsty Tonsil without them and if he suddenly showed up wearing them, questions might be asked. From here on he would have to be careful. He wanted to get out of the country now and away from Flea Hill and the Double J as soon as possible. Logan went to the railroad water tank on the other side of the tracks. Underneath the tank he checked the secret pouch in his belt, and to his surprise, he found that his $180 was still there. Leaving the money in his belt for safekeeping, the 'breed hid his weapon and belts and returned to the streets.

Since Jarting was in town, Other Day would have to lie low until he left. If he was seen by the ranch owner, he'd be in trouble for certain. Once Jarting left, Logan could get the dun mare and ride back to the ranch, get his bay gelding, and be on his way, if he wanted.

The half-breed hid in a shadowy passageway between two buildings from where he could see the hitching rail at the Thirsty Tonsil. He suddenly had a thought. What if the men and or Jarting stayed in Flea Hill all night? The next day was Sunday and they might want to continue raising hell until they had to go back to the ranch on Monday morning. He'd have almost to disappear to hope for an opportunity to get the mare in order to leave town without being seen. Maybe the men would bed down for a while and he'd have the chance if that happened.

Logan had no intention of interfering with Jarting's scheme. Why should he? He had no stake in the outcome of Jarting's plan, one way or the other. If Jarting wanted to cheat his way into a bigger ranch, it was of no concern to Other Day Logan. He had no sympathy for the Indians. If they were stupid enough to be led around the way Jarting was planning, they deserved to get whatever came out of the ruse.

Stupid Indians? His mother had been a Pawnee princess. As far as he knew, the Pawnees had never once been at war with the white man. Relations had always been well tended by both sides. Still, he knew the frustrations of being used by the white man because of his mother's fate. Half-Ear Hantelmann had turned his mother into a whore when his father died. She needed money in order to raise her son in the white man's world. Without the protection his father had offered when he was alive, she suddenly found herself on the outside of the white man's world looking in.

Was that any reason to try to help the Utes? Why should he even try? They'd not believe him anyway. If there was the chance of free whiskey to help them forget their plight of living on a reservation, they'd take it. And if the Utes thought they could do something to escape the miserable reservation, there'd be little Logan could do to dissuade them from trying it.

Without warning, thoughts of Mary Ann Hyburger suddenly filled his mind. Was she involved in this? Was she aware of her stepfather's plan? Did she approve? What if Jarting's crooked idea were discovered? Would Mary Ann be drawn in and punished along with Jarting? Would Jarting even be punished? Logan had no idea. Still, he wouldn't want to see an innocent person unjustly accused of something in which she'd had no part.

He knew that feeling. He'd just suffered it under the hand of Sheriff Ivo Turner. If he hadn't had the opportunity to escape, he might very well have had his neck stretched for horse stealing.

He wondered if Avery Longcamp knew what was going on. Maybe he should ask him. Maybe Avery would know if Mary Ann was involved. He doubted if the cowhand would know much of anything because men like Jarting seldom made mistakes like letting too many people know about their plans. If Avery couldn't answer his question, he'd ask Mary Ann herself, since he wanted to spare her the trouble of being pulled into Jarting's plans without her knowing them or the consequences of his actions if he were caught.

The 'breed leaned back against the building, all the time keeping his unwavering attention on the door of the saloon across the street.

As the hours passed, he watched most of the hands from the Double J come out with one of the whores and make their way in one direction or the other on the street toward the house where the woman lived. When Avery came back, looking worn out, leaning on Suellen, a smile crossed the 'breed's grim mouth. He wondered if he looked as silly when he quit the presence of one of the fallen angels.

A short time later, the door opened and a gang of men came out. He recognized them as the Double J ranch hands. Josiah Jarting was with them. They all mounted their horses and turned to leave. No one seemed to notice the mare Other Day had ridden into town, which was still tied at the far end of the rail. They turned their horses' heads and rode down the street, unmindful of the late hour and making no effort to cover their departure. A couple of them fired their six-guns in farewell to the town and the night's festivities.

When they were out of sight, Other Day moved back into the shadows. He'd go to the end of the street and cross there to the other side. He didn't want to run the risk of confrontation with the sheriff or deputy. Even though he felt certain they wouldn't recognize him in the dark, as they hadn't when they walked right by him in the saloon, he didn't want to take any chances.

Once he had his horse, he'd pick up his .44 and belt and follow the others back to the ranch.

Fifteen minutes later, he rode out of Flea Hill toward the west.

CHAPTER ELEVEN

Other Day walked the mare, and the animal, as if sensing the importance of making no noise, seemed to float across the turf toward the east side of the Jarting barn. By keeping the structure in front of him, the 'breed ensured that no one looking in that direction would detect his approach. Despite the fact that it was several hours past midnight, a moving figure would not be that difficult to see.

He swung out of the saddle when he pulled back on the reins, and the mare stopped with her head almost touching the wall. After laying the reins across the sill of an open window, he moved toward the corner to his right, from where he would be able to see almost all of the yard and the other buildings of the Double J.

Other Day had followed the ranch hands and

Josiah Jarting about 15 minutes or so after they rode out of Flea Hill. Now, the men who had opted to sleep out of doors were just about ready to lie down in their bedrolls for a few hours sleep before they had to get up. Maybe Jarting was trying to pull some sort of under-the-table deal, but at least he allowed his men to observe a day of rest when the time of year and work schedule allowed. Sunday would give the men time to recoup their strength from Saturday night's drinking and hell raising and give them a fresh start Monday. The horses used by the cowboys slowly milled about in the horse corral off to Other Day's right. Then, his body itched and he pressed against the wall. Was someone coming or was he about to be seen?

From where he stood, concealed by the barn, Logan could make out the movements of a shadowy figure, and almost at the same time, a light flickered in the ranch house, which was the farthest building from the 'breed's hiding place. The 'breed watched the man walk toward the corral. He took a saddle that had been straddling the top rail of the fence, where he had apparently put it minutes before, and entered the closure. The horses responded by moving about trying to avoid the intruder. After singling out a horse, he threw the saddle across the animal's back and quickly finished with a bridle over the head. Once the latigos were pulled tight, he mounted the horse and rode him out of the corral, reaching down to close and secure the gate. He rode away from the ranch in the direction of Flea Hill.

A few minutes later, the ranch house went dark.

Other Day frowned. What had that been all about? He hadn't been able to make out the face of the man who rode away, but from his height, Other Day was willing to bet that the man had been Shorty Enser. Where the hell was he going at that time of night? The men on the ground hadn't made any gestures or motions that would have indicated that they were not aware of what he was doing. They must have known what it was all about.

Crouching down, the 'breed waited almost half an hour until he was sure the men were sleeping before he moved from his place of concealment. He'd have to risk approaching Avery Longcamp to find out what was going on. Other Day's body continued itching, but not as intensely as it did when danger was close at hand. Avery's statement at the Thirsty Tonsil had almost convinced Other Day that the man had completely changed his attitude about the 'breed. Avery seemed to measure a man's stature as a man by the way he fought. Other Day had bested him, and Avery apparently admired a man capable of doing something like that. Now, the 'breed would have to run the risk that his interpretation was correct and talk with the cowboy.

When he felt certain the other men were all sound asleep, he moved out and away from the barn. His bay gelding, one of the horses in the corral, sensed his presence and moved to the rail fence, nickering softly. The 'breed walked over to him and patted him on the nose, quieting him. When he felt the horse would not make enough noise to betray his presence, he moved away from the corral.

He hoped that Avery was a man of habit and would be lying where he normally did. Crouching, the 'breed examined the face of the snoring man when he stood over a sleeping form. Convinced that it was Avery, Logan clamped a hand over his mouth and brought his right knee and leg across the sleeping man's left arm. Other Day's hand shot out and grabbed the man's right wrist.

Avery's snoring stopped immediately, but the other men continued their heavy breathing, their sleep undisturbed.

Avery's eyes widened and he struggled. When he was unable to free himself, he stopped wiggling about to recoup his strength for a new attempt.

"Shhhh," Other Day said quietly. "It's me, Logan."

When Longcamp heard Logan's voice, he relaxed and nodded, showing the 'breed that he knew who was pinning him to the ground.

"Don't make a sound. I've got to talk with you."

Avery nodded again and Other Day released his hold. He stood and moved away and Avery got to his feet and followed.

When they stood at the east side of the barn, Other Day turned and said, "What do you know about Jarting?"

"Whatcha mean?" Avery asked, smacking his lips and trying to rid his mouth of the stale taste of long-since-drunk whiskey.

"You've been working for him for less than a year, is that right?"

Avery nodded.

"As far as you know, is he honest?" Other Day knew better, considering what he had learned that night by eavesdropping outside the sheriff's office, but he had to know what Avery thought. Was Jarting covering his steps so well with the men that he saw every day? Or was he so confident that he didn't care if everyone knew what his plans were?

"I reckon. Why the hell you wakin' me up to ask me somethin' like thet for?"

"I have reason to believe that Jarting and the sheriff are hooked up in something that might cause some killings."

"What the hell you talkin' about, Logan?"

"I happen to know—"

"Say," Avery said, as if his head were being cleared of the cobwebs, "just a minute. What the hell you doin' here? J. J. sent Shorty back into Flea Hill to tell Ivo Turner that you're in town."

"I'm not, am I? I'm here. Why'd he do that?"

"He knows who you are."

Other Day smiled in the dark. "Oh? Who am I?"

"Some wild killer named Other Day Logan. Is that you?"

Other Day felt his itching lessen even more. Could he trust this man? Would Avery be trustworthy enough to help the 'breed in some way or other, to stop the bloodshed that was sure to come if Jarting put his plan into action? His instincts seemed to tell him he could. He had to risk it. In answer to Avery's question, the 'breed nodded. "I am Other Day Logan. I hope I can trust you, Avery."

"Shucks, you can trust me all right. But I'll say

this, you don't come across like no wild-eyed killer. Say, how'd you get sech a name?"

"A mix-up, that's all. But I'm not a killer."

"J.J. seems to think you are."

"How'd he decide that?"

"He was tellin' us on the way home about this Other Day Logan and how Ivo Turner let some Injun get away without all his knives and six-gun. Then, Bob Burgmeier recollected how you came ridin' in light with just a Winchester. Seems the Injun managed to get his horse and rifle before he left Flea Hill. So Jarting thinks you're this guy."

"Well," Other Day said slowly, "I've got my .44 now. You and I had a difference once. You still feel in a bad way toward me?"

"Hell no. When you and me talked in the Thirsty Tonsil, it wasn't the liquor talkin'. I meant what I said."

"Can I count on you for some help?"

"What kinda help?"

"I don't know if I'll need you or not, but in case I should, can I count on you?"

"Depends. Tell me about it."

"Jarting and Turner are mixed up together in something that could cause the deaths of a lot of innocent people. Jarting is trying to get rid of the Utes. I'm going to try to head off the trouble." Other Day launched into an account of the two conversations he'd overheard—one by accident when he tried to conceal himself from being seen by the lawman, and the other by design to satisfy his own growing curiosity.

When he finished, Avery shook his head and grunted. "Well, I'll be—"

"Do you know if Miss Mary Ann is tied up with him?"

"Hell's fire, I didn't even know what you just told me. I got no idea about that, but I sorta doubt it."

"Why?"

"I don't know her at all, but she don't seem the type. Of course, neither does old man Jarting. Say, you know that she's got eyes for you?"

Other Day looked intently at the man's shadowed face and laughed quietly. "I doubt that. She hasn't said more than a half-a-dozen words to me since I brought her in after the accident."

"It's the truth, Logan. I've seen her peekin' and spyin' on you ever since you took on here. 'Specially since the buckboard threw her."

The phantom image of Belle Doolin flashed through his mind. Mary Ann Hyburger might be an attractive woman, but in his estimation, she couldn't begin to compare with Belle—alive or dead. "I've got no time for that sort of thing now, Avery. Still, I should talk with her to see if she is aware as to what's going on. Do you know where she sleeps in the house?"

Avery squeaked out a laugh. "I thought you said you ain't got time for that?"

"I got to talk with her, and if Jarting is suspicious of me, he might order you men to capture me if they see me. If I'm going to talk with her, I've got to do it now, before the rest of the ranch wakes up. It'll be light in another couple of hours and I should be long gone by then." Other Day waited impatiently, sure his words had carried the urgency of which he wanted Avery to be aware.

"Oh, I see." Avery didn't continue.

When Other Day realized the ranch hand wasn't going to say anything else, he said, "Well do you know where she sleeps?"

"I think there's two bedrooms and they're both in back of the house next to each other. So I guess you can't see her now, can you?"

"Why not?"

"J.J.'ll hear you for sure."

"I'll have to make a noise first, and I don't intend on doing that." An air of confidence hung on each word.

"Be careful, Logan. You hear? Sounds to me like you're puttin' your nose in where it ain't wanted. If you don't get caught, you got nothin' to gain, and if you do get caught, you got everythin' to lose."

"You're right enough about that, Avery."

"Why the hell you doin' it then?"

"Good question. I don't know. Maybe it has something to do with the two bloods I got in me."

"I was wonderin' if you might be a 'breed. I guess it might make some sense if that's the way it is."

"That's the way it is;" Other Day said, "but it still doesn't make sense to me. I shouldn't have poked my nose into the things going on in Bell's Town either, but I did. 'Course there, I was pulled in and made to look like a fool. I don't like that. I guess maybe that was why I got involved there. Then, the woman I loved was dishonored and killed by the man who took over as sheriff in Bell's Town, and I had to kill my way through quite a few men to get at him."

"Did you kill him, too?"

Other Day nodded. "Yeah. I did."

"Well, dang it all, you be careful when you go pokin' around the house. Other than John Henry, ain't none of the hands supposed to go anywhere near it unless they been told to go there."

"Don't worry, I'll be careful. Can you unsaddle the mare I rode to town and get my gelding ready?"

"Sure."

"Just be quiet so no one hears you. Just talk to the bay and he won't act up. When he's ready, bring him here and put him in the same place where the mare is now."

"I understand."

"Then go back to sleep."

Other Day turned and walked off in the direction of the ranch house without making a sound. He crossed the footbridge and went to the front door. He hoped the door wasn't locked, and when tried, he found that it wasn't. Lifting on the door to keep its weight off the hinges and thus prevent any squeaking, Logan stepped inside. He immediately heard Josiah Jarting's snoring. That was good of the rancher. At least, Other Day knew which room not to investigate. After several seconds, his eyes adjusted and he made his way through the large living room without a sound.

He found the bedroom doors side by side and both were closed. He opened the one that would lead to Mary Ann Hyburger's bedroom and lifted it as he had the front door. He stepped inside and waited. He could hear the woman's steady breathing and knew she was in a deep sleep. That was good, but the 'breed hoped she wouldn't awaken too quickly and make a lot of noise doing so.

Testing each board he stepped on before putting all his weight down, Other Day laboriously made his way across the room toward the bed. When he was halfway there, Mary Ann suddenly turned in her sleep, and he stood statue-like, ready to drop to the floor if she gave any indication of awakening.

Mary had been lying on her side and now rested on her back. Once her breathing resumed its steady rhythm, he stepped forth again, moving toward the sleeping woman.

After several minutes, he stood next to the bed and noticed the graying of the blackness outside. A few birds began chirping their wake-up songs, and he knew he had less time than he had thought. Perhaps the birds would awaken both the woman and Jarting. He hoped they wouldn't. He'd have to run and wouldn't find out what he wanted to know. If he had any sense, he'd leave right then. But because he didn't want to see the Utes taken advantage of or any white people slaughtered by the red men, he had to do whatever he could to stop the blood letting Josiah Jarting wanted to start.

Dropping into a crouch, he reached out and clamped a hand over the woman's mouth. Startled, she tried to sit up, but when he held her down, she momentarily relaxed.

"Shhhh, Miss Hyburger. It's me, Logan. I've got to talk to you. Will you follow me outside? It's very important."

She managed to nod enough to tell Other Day that she would.

"You aren't going to scream out if I take my hand off your mouth, are you?"

She shook her head and he narrowed his eyes, studying as best he could the woman's facial expression in the dull gray light. He thought he detected a look of truth in her eyes and felt her relax completely. Recalling what Avery had said, he had to bank on the fact that she was interested in him and might think that his overtures were of a totally romantic nature.

"I'm going to take my hand off your mouth and go outside and go across the bridge. As soon as I'm out there, I want you to follow me. Will you?"

She nodded and Other Day thought she did so eagerly. He slowly removed his hand, keeping it in position to cover her mouth again if she decided to yell out. She didn't, and he stood and moved like a ghost across the room and out into the living room.

When he stepped onto the porch, he quickly made his way to the bridge and crossed it. He turned and saw the woman following him, a robe covering her nightdress.

She hurried across the foot bridge and walked up to him. "I like your new haircut."

Taken off guard, Other Day said, "How'd you know?"

"I watched Pancake cut it before you went to town. Did you have fun in town?" She smiled and tilted her head to one side.

"Miss Hyburger," Other Day said, again

recalling what Avery had said about her spying on him, "this isn't what you may think it is. I've got to ask you some very serious questions."

She frowned and studied his face. "Serious questions concerning what?"

"Concerning your stepfather."

She motioned for him to follow her and she walked toward a small copse of trees that stood 50 feet away. Once they were inside and out of sight of the ranch house, she said, "It's better if we're in here. I don't think Josiah will be up for a while, but we shouldn't be seen together like this. Ask your questions, Logan."

"Before I do, I want to tell you what I happened to overhear in the barn." He told her in a brief way, everything he'd heard Jarting and the sheriff talking about. When he finished, he said, "Were you aware of any of this?"

She smiled and said, "I could say no and find out everything you know and then tell Josiah. Or I could say yes and have you think I'm involved as well. Well, I didn't know any of it. That worthless, no good bastard. Let me tell you about him, Logan. He married my mother when I was about nine years old. I told you I was a baby when my Daddy died. Josiah had been the foreman, and he began sweet-talking my mother and pretty soon they got married. It wasn't long before he was running the whole ranch without asking my mother anything. Her health began to go bad and when he changed the brand from her Rocking H to the Double J, it about killed her. She died six months later."

"Why do you hang on here?"

"I've got no place to go, no family or friends to speak of. Since he's got the whole ranch running the way he wants it to, he doesn't care what I do around here as long as it don't interfere with him. But I can't believe that he's trying to get the Indian reservation land southwest of here. And the way you say he's going about it—" She shuddered.

"I guess you were too small and young to stop him when he was taking over," Other Day said matter-of-factly.

"All I remember was him saying he could run the ranch better if it was in his name. At the time, it made sense to me. Now, I can see that it was all part of a big plan he had. That—"

"Well, blood is going to flow if he succeeds in putting his plan into action."

"What can I do to help?" she asked, staring directly into the 'breed's eyes.

"Be ready to back up my story with your story of how he got control of your mother's ranch. Between the two of us, we might be able to convince the authorities that he's trying to steal the Indian's land."

"But Ivo Turner is in cahoots with him."

"I'm talking about the Army. Jarting intends to use the Army to move the Indians off the reservation. We're going to have to convince them of the truth."

"What are you going to do now? Go to the Army?"

"No, Miss. I'm going to the Indians. Maybe I can convince them that Jarting is a crook and trying to cheat them."

"But if Josiah has been stirring them up, won't

that be dangerous for you?"

"From what I know, there's only about twenty or so who are in contact with Jarting and Turner. If I can convince the Chiefs of the reservation, they'll take care of the renegades themselves, and the problem might be completely avoided."

"Do you know where the reservation is?" she asked.

"About twenty miles due south and west of here. Is that right?"

"Yes, beyond Twin Springs. Our land borders the reservation. I guess Josiah thinks that's the only way he can expand. There's ranches to the north and south and civilization east of us."

"This Twin Springs, what's that?"

"Two springs that are near each other and feed Stinky Creek. What are you going to do when you get to the Indians?"

Other Day didn't want to tell her about his own mixed heritage and open a corral full of questions that didn't have anything to do with the problem at hand. "I guess I'll try to talk some sense into them."

"What you're doing is dangerous, Logan. I'm scared for you."

"Don't be. I can deal with the Indians."

"You better come back, you hear?"

Other Day turned and walked away toward the barn, where the bay gelding waited. It was already too light to suit him. If anyone saw him riding away from the ranch, a posse might be sent out after him, and that would end any hope of his changing the outcome of the bloodbath Josiah Jarting wanted.

He could feel Mary Ann's eyes on him as he crossed the yard. He wanted nothing to do with her, and he'd tell her as soon as the time was right. No matter what the outcome of his visit with the Indians might be, he wanted no part of the notions she had in her head.

CHAPTER TWELVE

Long shadows stretched to the west as the sun eased over the horizon behind Other Day. He had left Stinky Creek and Twin Springs far behind. A breeze from the north and west slipped around him and he knew it would be a nice day. He hoped his efforts with the Utes would work out.

The gelding walked without hurrying, and Other Day realized that he should take it easy on the animal since he might need all the energy the horse could muster to make a hurried departure. He had no idea how much Jarting had stirred up the Indians. Were the Indians ready to lash out at anyone? Would they attack the white man without provocation? Would a half-breed, such as himself, be treated as one of them or as a hated white? Were the Utes so excited that they would attack anyone who crossed their path?

The 'breed shook his head. He had no idea as to how to enter the reservation or if the white or red side would be favored. He could hope for either side without reservation. He could hate either side just as easily. Would he let his white blood rule his feelings or his Indian blood?

Since it had been white men who had tried to jail him and try him on false charges, he felt he should lean toward the Utes. But could he convince them that the white men with whom they were dealing were only after the Indians' land? Would the leaders of the Utes understand that they were going to be duped out of their reservation and moved someplace that they would probably not find to their liking?

He had never had much to do with the Utes, but he had spent one winter with the Shoshoni, a people closely related to the Utes. If Other Day was lucky, and the Utes would be like the Shoshoni he knew, he had to do but one thing: convince the chiefs of the Utes not to take the whiskey and guns that Jarting had bought with money stolen from the stagecoachs and banks. If the Utes accepted the contraband, women and children on both sides would be hurt and killed, and Other Day did not want that to happen. If only braves and white men were killed, he'd have no argument. Let them kill each other. It would make for a better world if they did and it would make no difference to Other Day Logan.

Without stopping the gelding, Logan turned in his saddle and looked at the rising sun. He estimated that it would take about three hours total to walk the bay to the reservation. He had been riding for over an hour, which meant he should arrive at the Indian village about mid-morning. He turned back to face the front. At least his body wasn't itching. More than likely it would before he reached the Ute's reservation.

He wondered why the Indian agent wasn't doing anything about the situation. But, on second thought, the 'breed doubted that the agent would be able to do anything even if he knew about the impending crisis.

The bay continued his plodding walk, and two hours later, Other Day slowed him when he came to a saddleback rise. He smelled smoke on the air and could see it rising beyond the hill in front of him.

Logan dismounted and ground tied the gelding. Making his way forward, he dropped to his belly and continued until he could see into the valley below. He estimated that 150 crudely built tipis dotted the broad valley. A grim smile crossed his lips. They were not constructed to be permanent dwellings, such as the earthen lodges the Pawnee Indians built. The half-breed had only been in one of the Pawnee lodges once and had never gone back to his mother's people again. They had ostracized his mother, and he had removed them from his mind as if they no longer existed. But their domed lodges, made of earth with a shelf running around the interior, were well constructed and very warm and snug in the winter, much more so than the flimsy huts below.

Well, the 'breed had to go down sometime and it might just as well be right then. He scrambled backward and stood when he thought no one would see him in the valley below. After mounting the bay, he rode forward.

His body itched mildly as he rode into the village. Ute children stopped doing their chores or playing and watched him as he rode past. Squaws looked up, trying to show as little interest in the intruder as possible. But it was the braves that Other Day kept his eye on without being obvious. They stood, barely moving, with their faces toward him at all times. When he passed one, he knew he was being scrutinized, and only when he had passed, did the braves move and start to follow him. He wanted to turn in his saddle and look, but he knew they were gathering behind him, cutting off that avenue of escape. Despite the presence of the braves behind him, his itching didn't increase, and he felt reasonably safe for the moment.

Logan rode toward the center of the lodges, when he saw a group of five men confronting him, he reined back on the gelding. The chiefs of the village faced him, and Logan wondered if they were the men with whom he should speak and if there were more villages on the reservation than that one. From what he knew, the reservation was a small plot of land; so he was probably in the only village. And if there were no other villages, the leaders in front of him might be the same with whom Jarting was dealing. He'd know for sure in a few minutes.

With his right hand held up in the sign of peace, Logan dismounted. When he dropped the reins, the bay stood still. "How?" he said, his face remaining immobile, his right hand still held up in the sign of peace.

"How?" the oldest of the five leaders said.

Using a combination of Shoshoni words that he knew and sign language, Other Day asked, *"Are you the leaders of the village?"*

The old man nodded. *"What does a white man want here?"* he asked, using the same combination as Other Day.

The 'breed shifted his weight from one foot to the other, but before he could speak, the old man said, *"You are not white, but you are not a brave either. What are you? Are you of us or of the white man?"*

"Some of me is of you. My mother was a Pawnee princess."

"I have heard of them."

"My father was a white man who hunted and traded with the Pawnee."

"What are you called, Man-of-both? I am Quo-keta."

Other Day smiled to himself. Why tell him his full name. He would spend the rest of the day trying to explain the concept of baptism and how a wrong answer to a simple question had resulted in his unusual name. It would be best to keep everything simple and focus the conversation on his reason for being there. *"I am called Logan."*

"What do you want of the Utes, Man-of-both Logan?"

Other Day launched into as simple an explanation as he could, telling the chiefs of Josiah Jarting's duplicity and how the Utes, no matter what they did, would lose.

Quo-Keta watched Other Day closely. When the 'breed stopped, he said, *"I do not understand the words of the one called Man-of-both Logan."*

Other Day did not answer right away, but began reformulating in his mind the case he wanted to make. He knew the old chief knew and understood more than he was willing to admit. He wanted the 'breed to tell him three, four, maybe even five times the reason for his entry into his village, waiting for him to make some sort of slip up in the details. A sudden movement to his right caught Other Day's attention, but he didn't move his head. Only his eyes moved and his body tingled with a warning.

A tall, well-muscled brave stepped forward and faced the chiefs for a long moment, then turned to Other Day. *"You are not friend of the Utes,"* he said in sign language.

Other Day studied the man before him. The man's eyes bore into the 'breed, and Other Day knew he was face to face with the one who had been dealing with Jarting. This brave was the obstacle Other Day had to overcome. When the brave moved his skin rippled with muscles and a lean, hard look clung to his face, giving the otherwise handsome features an appearance of hatred and treachery.

"Why does He-who-interrupts say this without knowing the speaker?" the 'breed asked.

"You condemn Jar-ting when all he does is try to help us."

"Jo-si-ah Jar-ting wants your land to graze many cattle."

The brave's hands exploded with four words. *"You have two tongues."*

Before Other Day could make a retort, Quo-keta

stepped forward and laid a hand on the brave's shoulder. *"Little Eyes must not speak for the chiefs."* He turned to Other Day. *"Are the words of Man-of-both Logan true words?"*

Other Day nodded. *"It is as I have spoken, Quo-keta, Chief of the Utes. Are not the Utes here of the Snake Nation and close brothers of the Shoshoni and the Bannock?"*

"Yes, that is true."

"Are not the Utes of the Wind River Shoshoni?"

The old man nodded. *"Yes."*

"And the Bannocks of the Snake Nations are just like the Utes and Paiutes?"

"The same blood flows through their veins as flows through ours," Quo-keta said.

Little Eyes moved to one side, but kept his baleful stare fixed on Other Day.

Although the 'breed seemed to keep his attention fixed on the old chief, he never allowed Little Eyes out of his view. *"Many winters ago, the great White Father who lives where the sun rises gave to the Bannock people and to many Shoshoni the Fort Hall Reservation many days ride to the north. When the buffalo died off and the hunting went bad, there was no food. The Bannock and some of the Shoshoni rose up in anger. They left their home to find better hunting for their people. The great White Father's big knives drove them back to their reservation. This unhappy failure took place just nine moons ago."* Other Day paused, letting the story sink into the minds of the Chiefs and elders.

Before Quo-keta could speak, Little Eyes stepped forward again. *"You mix in things not your business, half-breed."*

"Little Eyes will be silent. It is not in his place to be speaking of these things now," Quo-keta said. He turned to Other Day. *"I know of the sad story you tell. But Jar-ting is said to be helping us. He has offered Little Eyes guns and whiskey."*

Other Day shook his head. *"It is wrong to take them. Only trouble will follow the Utes."*

Quo-keta smiled, showing an almost toothless mouth. *"With guns, we can defend ourselves when we go north."*

"Why do the Utes want to go north?" Other Day narrowed his eyes.

"To find better hunting."

"Is not the hunting good here?"

"It is good, but not as good as Jar-ting says it is in the north country."

"Jart-ting lies. Big knives will drive you back here or to another place that will make you and your people unhappy—some place far distant from here."

"Why would they do this, Man-of-both Logan?"

"I told you before that many crimes and wrongs have been done. The white men say the Utes have done these things."

"That is lie. Man-of-both Logan lies," Quo-keta said menacingly.

"I do not lie. I tell Quo-keta the chief what other white men say. These men will tell the big knives, and the big knives will believe them. Jar-ting wants your land here on the reservation." Other Day made a sweeping gesture with his left arm. His right arm hung down, his hand close to the .44. *"Jar-ting will lie to cheat you and your people out of it. But he will do it in such a way that the big*

knives will be hated by your people and he will be liked."

Little Eyes stepped back and stood between his chief and Other Day. *"He-of-the-mixed-blood is a liar and speaks with two tongues. He-of-mixed-blood is not a friend of the Utes."*

Other Day stared at the brave. Seldom had he seen such hatred focused on him by another. He wondered if his own hatred for Ike Furlong had come close to matching the venomous loathing he was receiving from the Ute brave? Ike had killed Belle and Other Day had killed Ike. Even after the murderer was dead, Logan had continued choking him, only when the citizens of Bell's Town had pulled him off the corpse, had he started to simmer down a little. But that anger, that ultimately fulfilled hatred, was justifiable because of what had been done. Little Eyes had no reason that Other Day knew about to hate him or the whites, yet an all-consuming detestation seemed to rule and dominate the man completely.

"Little Eyes," Quo-keta said ominously, *"is speaking for his chiefs again. He runs the risk of facing the council once Man-of-both Logan leaves. Go from us now or be punished later."*

Little Eyes, his hatred intensifying even more because of the humiliating reprimand, glared at Other Day and then stormed away.

Quo-keta faced Other Day. *"Man-of-both Logan, go now. The chiefs and council will talk of what Man-of-both Logan has said."*

"I came here in peace and I leave here in peace, Quo-keta. When you and your council talk, remember that many of your squaws and young

could be killed the same as the Utes would kill the white man's women and children." Logan held up his right hand again and then turned to the bay. He picked up the reins and led the gelding away from the center of the village. He'd mount once he was clear of the dwellings since he wanted to appear as calm and in control as he had when he arrived. If the bearer of the words that the chief and council were going to mull over appeared frightened, they would give little heed to the warning.

When he had only two more tipis to pass, the bay suddenly reared and Other Day's body began itching violently. Little Eyes leaped from the shelter of the second last structure and faced the 'breed, his knife drawn.

"Stay out of this, Mixed-blood. You are a half-breed and know not the ways of either the red man or the white man. You know nothing." His voice growled the Shoshoni words, and his sign language appeared as hostile gestures and threats.

"Why should I stay out of it, Little Eyes?"

"It is none of your business."

"Since I walked from the center of the village, have you become chief over Quo-keta?" Other Day made the statement as bitter and sarcastic as possible.

"I'm the leader of those who meet with Jar-ting. we have the ears of the chief and the council."

"Do you want your women and children slaughtered? Are you nothing more than a killer of women and children yourself? That is not much for a brave to be proud of." Other Day narrowed his eyes again and glared back at the Ute. He found

he could hate the Indian almost as easily as he had ever hated anyone in his life.

"Stay out, Mixed-blood, or I will kill you next time we meet!"

Other Day mounted the bay and looked down at the brave. "Sure you will," he growled in English. He clucked to the gelding and the animal started forward at a trot. The 'breed didn't turn back because doing that would show he was concerned about the threat Little Eyes had made. By not looking back, he hoped the brave realized he believed the threat to his life hollow. Still, the 'breed knew it was no hollow threat. He would have to be on his guard because it would be like the Ute to circle around to get in front of him and attack him when he was least expecting it.

The farther Logan rode away from the village, the less his body itched. For the time being, he felt he was safe. He coaxed the gelding more and the animal galloped. After 15 minutes, Other Day slowed the horse to a walk once more and continued riding east toward the Double J ranch.

Almost three hours later, Other Day reined up and turned the bay into a small valley. He was only four miles away from the Double J and the sun was still up. Turning in the saddle, he looked at the western horizon. It would be at least three or four hours before it would be dark. He would have to wait another hour or two beyond that to allow the ranch to quiet down for the night.

The 'breed yawned. He didn't know how long it had been since he had slept for more than a few minutes at the same time. After he left the Ute village, he had dozed in the saddle, but that had been merely a stopgap measure. And he hadn't slept at all the night before when he returned to the ranch from Flea Hill. But if he didn't stop Jarting, his sleepless nights would all be for nothing.

Once he was well within the valley, he pulled up and dismounted. The bay could use some rest, too. He fumbled in the saddlebags and found a couple of pieces of jerky. After he took the saddle off the gelding, he removed the bridle and hobbled the horse's hind legs. Inside a small copse of trees, he rested the saddle against one of the boles, then sat down, facing the way he had entered. He quickly devoured the jerky and then lay back with his arms over his face.

Within minutes he was sound asleep.

Instantly arising from the blackness that held Other Day's unconscious mind, Little Eyes leaped at him. In his sleep, the 'breed ducked to one side. The sonofabitch wanted to kill him. He had said that he would kill Logan the next time they met.

Awakening from his dream, Other Day sat up, his mind groggy from the depth of his sleep. He looked around in the deepening darkness for Little Eyes. Then he thought he heard something. It was a creaking sound of some sort. What the hell could that be? Slowly, the noise died away and was gone. Silence as deep as his sleep closed in around him.

Other Day shook his head. He had to start thinking more of himself and get better sleep. He didn't like to dream such things. It was bad enough that Little Eyes had threatened him, although that in itself didn't bother the 'breed. But the idea that he couldn't lie down for the night without having the threat replayed in his mind troubled him. Did that mean he had taken the menacing words seriously? Logan smiled ruefully as he pondered the innumerable times other men had threatened his life. It seemed that his very presence brought out the worse in most people—no matter what color the people. Almost every threat had turned out to be nothing more than empty words.

But Little Eyes was different somehow. He had had such hatred on his face and in his soul that Other Day knew his threat had been genuine. Logan would have to be extra alert during the next while because he knew the Ute would try to carry out his promise if they did meet.

Other Day lay back. Overhead, the stars were beginning to show. He'd sleep for another couple of hours, then make his way back to the ranch. He closed his eyes and forgot the Ute brave for the time being and concentrated on the peculiar noise he'd heard as he awakened. Logan couldn't decide if it or the dream disturbed his sleep.

Propping himself up on an elbow, he looked around the darkening valley. The bay was grazing no more than 60 or 70 feet away. Having dismissed the thought of the Ute attacking him for the time being, Other Day lay back and turned on his side. He closed his eyes and drifted off to sleep once more.

This time, he didn't dream.

CHAPTER THIRTEEN

Other Day rode slowly toward the Double J ranch through the dark night. An overcast sky blotted out the moon, and while he knew the darkness would conceal his approach, it also made for slow riding. But he had no reason to hurry.

Logan had slept for almost five hours and felt certain that everyone on the ranch would be asleep. Thus, his entry and presence would be that much easier to cover. The first thing he wanted to do was get to Avery. He wanted the man to be ready to help in whatever way he could.

Ahead, he could make out the dark, shadowy outlines of the ranch buildings in the gloom. Off to his left, he could hear the water flowing along the creek that passed through the ranch close to the main house. The 'breed turned the bay's head toward it, and when he was near, he crossed over to the far side to make certain that he was on the same side of the stream as the house.

When the half-breed came to the first tree that served as a windbreak around the ranch house, he pulled up and dismounted. He tied the bay to one of the trees and started through the grove. Once he had awakened and spoken to Avery, he would return to the ranch house and go to Mary Ann.

Other Day passed within 50 feet of the house, but used the shadows and trees to such advantage that anyone trying to see him from the house would have missed him. No noise issued from his feet, and when he had nothing but open space to cover between the last building and the bunk house area, he merely walked through, abandoning his pretense at sneaking. If someone awoke and saw Logan, he would think the 'breed was just one of the hands returning from the outhouse.

He checked the faces of those men sleeping outside, knowing he would find Avery among them. In a while, they'd have to start using the bunkhouse since it would be too cold to sleep outside anymore. When Logan stood over Avery, he crouched and touched him on the shoulder. The man stirred, but didn't awaken immediately. The 'breed shook him just a bit, and then before Avery could realize what was happening, Other Day clamped a hand over his mouth. His eyes opened wide, Avery strained to see who was holding and gagging him so effectively.

"Shhhh," the 'breed warned. "It's me, Other Day."

Avery relaxed and the 'breed released his hold.

"Where in tarnation you been?"

"I went to the Utes."

"What did you find out?"

"You'd better get up and follow me," Other Day said quietly. "I don't want to wake up the other men. Come on."

In minutes they stood behind the chuckhouse, away from the sleeping men. The could see the main house some 70 yards away.

"Jarting has them going pretty good," Logan said. "They're r dy to listen to anything he says, and they'll probably do whatever he says they should."

"That's bad, Other Day, real bad. We'd better get the soldiers from Fort Benecke-Berndt here pronto."

"How far away are they?"

"Thirty miles to the south of Flea Hill."

"Come on with me." Other Day stepped away and started toward the main house. He had his doubts about the Army—it might get there in time and it might not.

"Where we goin'?"

"I want to tell Mary Ann. She should know."

"Why?"

"She should get out of here and into Flea Hill. If the Indians attack, she'll be safer there."

"You think they'll attack the Double J?"

Other Day shrugged. "I don't know. but if I were Josiah Jarting and I wanted to get away with something like this, I'd let the Indians do whatever they wanted us to make it all look good and real."

"I don't follow you, Logan."

"If the Indians attack the ranch here and shoot

it up, killing a few hands and maybe burning some of the buildings, who's going to suspect Jarting of being behind the Utes burning him out?"

Avery shook his head. "Sure makes sense when you say it like that."

Other Day struck out for the house again, this time with Avery right behind him.

Halfway there, Avery said, "Say, Other Day, how come you don't make no noise when you walk?"

Other Day stopped. "Maybe it's my sneaky Indian blood. I don't know."

Avery chuckled and followed the 'breed toward the trees where the bay was tied.

"You wait here, Avery. I'll be back in a while with Miss Mary Ann."

Before Avery could answer, he found himself alone.

Other Day made his way to the front of the house and slipped inside without making a sound. When he stood in the middle of the main room, he stopped. Something was wrong, but he couldn't figure out what it was. He concentrated and then decided it was the lack of snoring. Was Jarting sleeping but not snoring? Or had he gone out to meet the Utes? If that were the case, Logan and Avery would have to move fast.

He strode toward the door to Mary Ann's room, still making no noise as he walked, and gently lifted the latch. He slowly opened the door and stepped in.

"Hold it right there! Don't move!" Mary Ann said shakily.

"It's—"

"Don't make a move, mister. I got you covered."

"—Logan," he finished.

"Logan? Thank God you got away from the Utes in one piece." Her voice sounded unsteady at first, but became stronger as the knowledge that the 'breed was back sank in.

"Where's Jarting?"

"Gone."

"Gone where?"

"He left around sundown. I think he's gone to meet the Utes."

Other Day frowned in the dark. "Did he go alone?"

"No. John Henry went with him. He must be in on this with Josiah."

"Sure seems that way. Come on outside with me."

"We can talk here all right. We're the only ones in the house."

Other Day thought he detected a note of invitation in the woman's voice, but decided not to say anything for fear he had misinterpreted her meaning and would embarrass her as well as himself if he said the wrong words. He felt she had more sense than to suggest something romantic when they were faced with a crisis. "Avery Longcamp is outside."

As if that were explanation enough, Other Day turned and left the bedroom. He heard Mary Ann follow him through the large room and the open door. When he turned he found her fully clothed, not in her night dress as she had been the previous night.

"Why is Avery Longcamp out here, Logan?"

"He's against what Jarting's doing."

When they reached the place where the 'breed had tied the gelding, they found Avery waiting for them.

"Avery?" Mary Ann said when they stood in the concealment of the trees.

"Yes, ma'am?"

"Did you see Josiah leave?"

"Yep, I sure did. That wagon was loaded with something other than the hay they had on it."

"Wagon?" Other Day asked.

"The one you greased real good the other day."

"Were they headed west?" the breed asked.

"They must have been," Mary Ann said. "When John Henry came to the house and told Josiah the wagon was ready, I heard Josiah say something about the sheriff and his deputy meeting them after dark at Twin Springs. Then John Henry asked when the Utes were going to show up, and Josiah said they'd be there shortly after dawn."

Other Day scowled. It was going too fast. Jarting had the advantage because his plan was almost operative, and the 'breed had no counteraction planned. What could they do to thwart it at this late stage? "Avery, you'd better get a horse and ride to Flea Hill. Wire the army at Fort Benecke-Berndt and tell them they're needed right now." Other Day turned to the woman. "Miss Mary Ann, you'd best go with him. I'm afraid if you stay now you'll be in real danger."

"Here at the ranch?"

"I don't think Jarting would hesitate to have the place burned and the men and maybe you shot if it meant the success of his plan. If you were to be taken prisoner by the Utes, you'd find their women can treat a white woman terribly."

Mary Ann slowly nodded. "I know. What are you going to be doing? Where are you going?"

"After the wagon. If Jarting's plan isn't stopped, there's going to be a lot of blood spilled on both sides. I have a double stake in this when you consider my own heritage, I guess. If we can get the army here in time, we can stop him. Maybe I can slow them down enough to give the Army the time it needs. You'd better wake the men. They should get out of here, too. They don't owe their lives to Jarting."

"You be careful, Logan. By the way, just what is your first name?" Mary Ann asked.

"Other Day, Miss Mary Ann. Other Day Logan."

"That's a strange name."

"Avery can tell you who I am on the way into town."

Mary Ann took a step toward Other Day and stopped. "You be careful, Logan."

"Come on, Miss Mary Ann," Avery said, a hint of urgency in his voice.

She started to follow him, then stopped and turned to the half-breed one more time. "You come back, Other Day Logan."

The 'breed nodded. "I will." He watched her disappear into the dark shadows of the trees behind Avery.

Turning to the bay, Logan untied the line that tethered the animal to a tree branch. He didn't like the sound of Mary Ann's request. Or had come back been an order? If she was serious about proposing some sort of deal with him, he wasn't the least bit interested. Maybe he was being overly cautious, but Avery had said he'd seen her watching Logan from time to time in a way that could only mean one thing. And Other Day wasn't interested in anything like that. Not that Mary Ann Hyburger wasn't an attractive woman. But he had no desire to settle down for even a week if it wasn't his idea in the first place. And there was always the ghost of Belle Doolin hovering in his mind.

He swung into the saddle and followed the stream back along the way he'd come earlier. He'd ride along the bank of Stinky Creek until he came close to Twin Springs; then he'd have to be careful. According to his internal clock, it was a couple of hours past midnight. He'd have to hurry to get the lay of the land, scout the camp that Jarting and the others had set up, and prepare to hinder their plan long enough to give the Army time to get there from the fort. He quickly calculated the quickest time the Army could get there. It would take Avery two to three hours to get into Flea Hill with Mary Ann along. Then, once the Army was aware of the problem and prepared to ride, it would take a detachment of soldiers close to five or six hours to reach Twin Springs, if they rode directly there. If Other Day failed, the Army would have to track the Utes.

What the hell could Other Day do to stop the Utes and Jarting? He'd have to wait until he reached Twin Springs before he decided on a plan.

After a while, his mind shifted to earlier in the night when he had lain down to sleep for a few hours. He had dreamt and then awakened to hear a strange noise. He replayed it in his mind and realized he'd heard the wagon. It must have creaked whenever the box of the Cooper vehicle twisted while going over the rough ground. The wheels weren't making any noise. Other Day had seen to that by doing such a good job greasing them.

For the next hour and a half, Other Day followed the bank of Stinky Creek at a slow pace. When he came around a hill that had prevented him from following the bank, he saw the glow of a campfire over the next low-lying hillock. He reined up and listened intently. He could just make out the voices of men. Twin Springs should be up ahead.

Logan had to be careful because the bay might whinny or the horses of the men up ahead might sense his gelding and begin neighing. Pulling on the reins, he turned the bay and rode back beyond the hill that had taken him away from the creek bank. A short distance past that, he found a small stand of oak trees and tied his mount there. Pulling the Winchester from its boot, he checked to make sure the magazine was full, then checked his Colt. A growl rumbled deep within him when he thought of his bowie knife and the other two blades that Jake Schuster had broken. He could use them now when he attacked the camp.

Other Day struck out toward the faint glow on the horizon and retraced his route to where he had stopped the gelding and then turned back. Ghost-like, Other Day passed through the night.

When Logan stood within 50 feet of the dying campfire, he realized that the deputy, Jake Schuster was sleeping while on guard. He could see the other three men had bedded down already. He listened and could hear the four men snoring.

So far, the situation was to his advantage.

The 'breed crept forward and, when he was behind Schuster, struck him across the back of the head with the butt of his rifle. The man fell to one side and Other Day smiled. That was for the knives. Leaning the rifle against the rear wagon wheel, he picked the man up and heaved him across his shoulder. Grabbing his rifle, he left the camp. When he came to a tree that was 25 yards away from the campfire, but still in full view of it, he dumped the deputy to the ground. He needed some rope and went back to the camp. He took the time to look in the wagon and saw case after case of rifles, boxes of small ammunition, and a dozen kegs of whiskey.

Logan stripped the rope off the brake and then found more on the seat of the Cooper wagon. He left the camp without making a sound and returned to the tree where he'd left Schuster. Tying the man's hands behind his back, Other Day fashioned a loop that caught the deputy's feet, then wrapped it around his neck. Finally he brought the rope back to the man's bound wrists and passed the end under them. He looked up and threw the long end over a branch that was no more than 10 feet off the ground.

He grabbed the rope and pulled, hauling Deputy Jake Schuster into the air. The deputy gurgled and choked as the rope tightened around his neck. His arms were pulled up and back, and they acted as a pulley for the rope garroting him.

When Schuster swung belly down about five feet off the ground, Other Day tied the rope to the trunk and moved away taking the deputy's .44

Army revolver. He wanted to be across the creek with the camp in full view in case the other three might awake by chance. The only sound Logan heard as he went to hide was the water gurgling in the two natural springs.

The 'breed took up a position behind a rock outcropping that would give him protection in the event the other three were able to return gunfire. He looked at the eastern horizon and figured he had about an hour before the sun would be up. Raising the Winchester, he drew a bead on the dying campfire and squeezed the trigger.

The shot echoed through the low hills, and the three men woke up and hurried to their feet, confused by the report. Flames leaped from the disturbed embers and the horses, tied to a tether line some 20 yards away, neighed and stirred around.

When Other Day heard the men asking what was going on, he smiled. Like buffalo waiting to be slaughtered, the men stood out in the open, their weapons on the ground next to their bedrolls, where they had placed them in the event they needed them during the night.

"God in heaven," Turner yelled. "Look!" He pointed toward the tree where his deputy had choked to death and still swung to and fro.

"Who did that?" Jarting asked. He looked around as if the devil himself might suddenly rise up from the ground before him.

Other Day had cocked the Winchester after he fired and now aimed at John Henry Lutehoser. Before he squeezed the trigger again, he yelled, "Jarting?"

Jarting whirled around trying to determine from where the voice had come. "Who's there? Speak up."

John Henry moved to get his six-gun, and Other Day allowed him to pick it up.

"Don't try to shoot that gun, John Henry, or you'll be in big trouble." Hadn't the foreman said something like that to the 'breed?

"Who is that?" Jarting asked. "Who's out there?"

"Nobody you'd care to know. I—"

Turner dove for his six-gun, and Other Day followed him with the barrel of the Winchester and squeezed the trigger just as the sheriff brought his gun up. The slug tore through the lawman's right shoulder; before the echo of the shot died away, Other Day had ejected the casing and drove a new shell in place.

Lutehoser brought his own six-gun up, but had no idea what to shoot at. Then by luck he took aim on the rocks behind which Other Day crouched. The 'breed saw him and aimed. When John Henry shot, Other Day did the same and the man fell back like a toppled sack of grain, a gaping hole between his eyes.

The sheriff had ducked behind Jarting, trying to hide, and when he came out from behind the rancher, Other Day squeezed off another round. Turner managed two more steps before he fell dead.

When Other Day checked for Jarting he found the man picking up his six-gun and putting it behind his back. Jarting boldly stood up, the revolver hidden behind him, and called out.

"Whoever you are, come out and let's talk. I know you're not one of the Utes. You're a white man. Come on. We can make a deal that will be good for both of us."

Other Day stood and stepped out from behind the rocks.

"Well, well, well. Logan. I never would have suspected it was you. What do you want? Why did you kill these men?"

"Don't try to play games with me, Jarting. I know what your plan is and I'm going to stop you."

"Why?"

"Because it's scurvy rabble like you who turn Indians into drunks and killers. Leave them alone, damn it."

"Why are you so interested? What have the Utes done for you?"

"I'm half Pawnee, and I hate white men who act like you. I hate Indians who let white men take advantage of them. I'm—"

Before Logan could finish the sentence, Jarting whipped his pistol out to blow the 'breed away. But Other Day was too quick. The Winchester came up, and he squeezed the trigger before Jarting could aim. The rifle spoke first, the slug tearing through Josiah Jarting's heart. Jarting's six-gun went off, sending the slug into the ground as the rancher winced and fell dead.

Other Day crossed the creek and entered the camp. He stepped over the dead men and went to the wagon. He had a lot to do before the Utes arrived.

He had to destroy the guns, the ammunition, and the whiskey. He could hitch the team up and try to get back to the ranch before the Utes caught him, but he knew that was impossible. Without a doubt, they'd overtake him with no touble.

Logan pried open the first case of rifles and found six weapons, cleaned and ready to fire. If all the arms were like that, he'd have to destroy them all. If they had been greased yet, it would take time for the Indians to clean them.

The 'breed heaved the case over the side of the wagon, then threw the rest of them out. They broke open when they hit the ground, and Other Day began smashing the butts against a boulder that rested against the base of the nearest hill. When he finished, he had 72 smashed Winchesters lying in a heap.

Carrying the ammunition over, he dumped the shells onto the pile. When he finished with that, he lugged the casks of whiskey to the pile and pulled the bung after working it loose. After sloshing the liquor over the rifles and shells, he returned and got another. Just as he finished dumping the last keg, he heard hoofbeats.

Logan had been so engrossed in his work he hadn't noticed the sun had risen. It was at least an hour after sunup, and the Utes were coming. He listened carefully and concluded that five or six horses were approaching.

Other Day picked up his rifle and walked away from the smashed contraband. Pulling out his headband—the headband his Pawnee mother had made long ago—he put it on. If he was ever able to think like an Indian or to convince other Indians that he was one of them, now was the time. He picked up a piece of wood from the fire, its ember still glowing, and blew on it. When a steady yellow flame danced on the end, he returned to the whiskey soaked rifles. Thrusting it in, he stepped back and waited until the wood stocks began smouldering. Then the 'breed walked to the creek bank and waited.

CHAPTER FOURTEEN

Other Day kicked a pebble to appear nonchalant when the Utes rode into view across a rise west of Twin Springs. He leaned the Winchester against a nearby rock and dropped his right hand close to the Colt .44 in the event that there would be gunplay at close quarters. Should that happen, he preferred his six-gun to the 15-shot rifle, but he had positioned his rifle behind a rock, which he could use for protection if the Utes gained the upper hand.

Logan glanced at the stack of smashed rifles and saw a column of smoke growing in density as the whiskey-soaked stocks and kegs caught fire. Once the flames were hot enough, the shells would begin exploding, taking the Utes off guard. The 'breed thought his preparations should give him the upper hand.

When the five horsemen neared, Other Day made out the figure of Little Eyes riding in the lead. Once they spotted the bodies of Jarting, Turner, and the others, the Indians pulled up short, the leader's horse rearing on his hind legs.

One brave saw the pile of rifles smoking and flames dancing on the ruined contraband. Little Eyes nodded when the brave called his attention to the fire, and after surveying the scene one more time, he turned to Other Day. *"What is the meaning of this? Has Mixed-blood done this?"*

Other Day stared at him, a grim expression on his face. The z-shaped scar flamed red as his anger for the stupidity of Jarting and the Indian confronting him rose. *"Mixed-blood has done this. Go back to your reservation and forget about a plan that is doomed before you begin. What Jar-ting wanted to do was wrong for the Ute as well as for the white-eyes."*

"Mixed-blood is not Ute. Mixed-blood is not white. He is between both the red man and the white eyes with no allegiance to either. When you left our village, I told you then that I would kill you the next time we met. Now is that time."

Little Eyes kicked his mount in the sides and the horse bolted forward. The Ute screamed out his hate-filled challenge to Other Day as he covered the distance separating them.

Other Day did not go for his six-gun, knowing he could draw it in the time it would take the horse to move one complete step. The 'breed waited to see what Little Eyes would do. Perhaps his actions were nothing more than a hollow gesture.

When the horse was ten feet from Other Day,

the Ute leaped from his mount's back and sailed through the air directly at the 'breed, a knife clutched in one hand.

Other Day cursed himself for not having drawn his .44, but it was too late for self-recriminations. He had to defend himself against the airborne Ute coming at him. Reaching out, Logan caught the wrist of the Indian's hand and took the full impact of the brave's weight as he crashed into the 'breed. The Indian pony charged by, grazing the falling duo, and Other Day, taking the full impact from the mount, fell to one side, the Ute hanging onto him with his left hand.

Other Day landed on his back, his adversary pulling himself up to straddle the 'breed's chest. Other Day clutched the Ute's right wrists, keeping the knife at bay while both men tried to end the confrontation one way or the other—Other Day by dislodging the Ute and going for his six-gun, and Little Eyes by plunging his knife's blade into the 'breed's heart.

Locked together, they struggled against one another until Other Day managed to get his weight and that of the Indian to sway from one side to the other. Once he had sufficient momentum, the 'breed rolled both of them to his left toward the water of Stinky Creek. The half-breed came up on top, his left hand on the throat of Little Eyes and his right hand pinning the brave's knife hand to the ground.

But the momentum he had built quickly worked against the 'breed, and Little Eyes managed to throw Other Day to his left, causing both men to drop three feet into the water. Just before going under, Other Day realized what was happening and took a quick breath. He held it as he found Little Eyes' weight forcing him to the riverbed bottom. He fought desperately to dislodge the Ute, but the man held firm while Other Day struggled relentlessly to free himself.

Still holding the Indian by the knife hand, Logan released his choke hold, quickly made a fist, and smashed it forward, directly at his adversary's throat. The 'breed felt the effect of his blow when the Ute stiffened and relaxed his grip on Other Day. His lungs burning from the short supply of air he had managed to suck in before going under, Other Day lashed out, hoping to strike Little Eyes hard enough to completely dislodge him.

The blow managed to catch the Ute off guard, and he toppled away from Other Day's chest. Gasping for air, the 'breed quickly launched his own attack. When he broke the surface of the water, Logan caught a swift glimpse of the Ute braves still astride their horses, waiting for the outcome of the battle. At least Other Day knew they wouldn't interfere because of Little Eyes' hatred and grudge against Other Day. It was up to the 'breed to dispatch the Ute troublemaker and make his point with the remaining Indians.

The 'breed caught Little Eyes around the neck with both hands, but had to release his left to ward off the knife as it swept toward him in a swinging arc. The underside of his left forearm caught under the wrist of the Ute, and the force of the collision opened the hand of Little Eyes, sending the knife flying to the shore. Realizing they were equally armed, Other Day didn't go for his Colt, but reared back and sent a fist flying at Little Eyes' mouth.

The Ute tried to duck, but took the full impact squarely on his nose and mouth. Blood spattered in all directions from his smashed nose and lips and his tongue, which was caught between his teeth and the intruding knuckles. Little Eyes fell toward the bank with his upper body on the ground and his legs still in the water.

Other Day plodded toward him, slowed by the water as it swirled about his legs. From where he lay, Little Eyes could see the knife within reach of his left hand. Grasping the weapon, he leaped to his feet and turned to face Other Day. Before the brave could bring his blade into play, the 'breed grabbed the Indian's knife hand with one hand and lashed out again with the other, catching Little Eyes with a glancing blow. Each man closed their arms around the other's upper body, seeking to gain an advantage. As they fought, they fell to the bank, their momentum carrying them out of the water and across the ground.

Both struggled to their feet and Little Eyes tried to kick Other Day, but the 'breed countered, blocking the Indian's foot with his own left and striking out with his right fist. He caught the Ute and sent him staggering backward toward the growing fire.

The 'breed, unmindful of the shells in the stack of burning rifles, followed up his attack with another series of blows. Little Eyes fell back farther and Other Day continued to pursue him.

The Ute kicked out with a foot again and caught

the 'breed in the groin. When Other Day fell to his knees, the Ute sensed he had his foe at a disadvantage and leaped forward with his knife poised over his head, ready to sink the blade into the heart of his adversary.

The 'breed, reacting to the Indian flying through the air at him, brought his fist up in a looping right-hand arc and caught Little Eyes on the side of the head again, causing the Indian to fall to the left of Other Day. The 'breed followed directly and landed on him, his groin still burning from the painful kick. But he knew he had to fight with all his energy because this was a fight to the death. For a split second he thought how Avery Longcamp would have enjoyed being in such a situation.

Other Day straddled the Ute's chest and tried to choke him, but the Indian swiftly brought the knife around and stabbed the 'breed's shoulder. The searing sensation of the blade slashing through muscle brought a yelp from Other Day, but the cry of pain quickly turned to a growl of hatred.

The peculiar sound took Little Eyes off guard, and Other Day clamped a hand over the man's face, two fingers digging into his eyes. The Ute retaliated by doing the same, his fingers digging into the 'breed's eyes. Then he jammed his thumb into Other Day's mouth, ripping at the cheek.

Again Avery Longcamp came to mind and Other Day clamped down on the intruding thumb with all his jaw's strength and felt the knuckle smash between his molars.

Little Eyes screamed, dropping the knife to help

pull his wounded hand from the 'breed's mouth. While his eyes were still blinded, Other Day bit down all the harder. The Ute pulled back as best he could, and when the 'breed could make out his head through his impaired eyes, he whipped another fist toward the Indian. This time he caught the Indian in the throat, then reared up with his body, and threw Little Eyes off.

Other Day scrambled to his feet and kicked at the Ute's head. Little Eyes fell backward toward the fire and Other Day followed. Before he could leap on his enemy, Other Day found the Ute on his feet and charging at him. The two men grappled and fell to the ground, rolling directly toward the fire. Little Eyes' hands closed on Other Day's throat, and the 'breed lashed out wildly but ineffectually trying to shake loose of the death grip.

His hands flailing about, his right closed by accident on the handle of the knife which the Indian had dropped. Other Day could feel the damp stickiness of his own blood as it matted his shirt at the shoulder. His vision grew muddled and spots of light flashed as the Ute continued choking him. He felt hot and then realized that the fire was inches from his face. The Indian choked him throwing his head from one side to the other, and the 'breed caught sight of several brass casings. *The shells!*

They could start going off any second once the fire was hot enough. Logan had to get free of Little Eyes and dispatch him. He swung wildly with the knife and heard the Ute scream. The choke hold released, Other Day's head swam for a moment as the blood rushed back. He gasped and heaved upward, throwing the Indian off him. Only wounded, Little Eyes charged Other Day again, but was met by his own knife as the 'breed brought it upward in an arc, the blade slipping between his ribs, tearing its way into the heart of Little Eyes.

Knowing he had won, Other Day let go of the knife, and the Ute fell forward onto his face. The 'breed turned and walked hurriedly toward the rock where his Winchester stood. He looked around as he walked, searching for his six-gun, which had been knocked from its holster sometime during the fight. He found it on the ground near the bank of the creek.

Picking it up, he dropped it in his holster and retrieved his rifle. Then, he turned to face the four Utes, who still sat astride their ponies.

"Go back to Chief Quo-keta. Tell him that Man-of-both Logan has killed Little Eyes. The Utes should stay on their reservation and be happy. Jarting is dead. His helpers are dead. There are no rifles. No bullets. No fire water. Do you understand?"

One of the braves, an expression of what appeared to be relief on his face, nodded. "*We will tell him. Man-of-both is a brave warrior. We will tell Quo-keta.*"

Just as the Utes turned their mounts, the first of the shells exploded and Other Day dropped down behind the rock nearest to him. The Utes kicked their ponies in the sides and rode as fast as they could, believing Other Day was firing at them.

The 'breed slipped into the creek and walked hunched over to keep from exposing his body to the wild shots coming from the direction of the fire he'd started. He continued walking that way until he was well out of range and away from Twin Springs. Scrambling out of the water, he made his way to the bay gelding and mounted. He turned the horse's head toward the Double J ranch and Flea Hill, where he would find Mary Ann Hyburger and Avery Longcamp.

The bleeding in his shoulder had long since stopped, but it pained him whenever he moved it. Still, the 'breed continued riding. Four hours later he walked the gelding down the only street in Flea Hill. He had no idea where Mary Ann or Avery might be. After he rode past the courthouse and jail, he came to the depot and stopped when the door burst open and Avery came charging out.

"Hey! Other Day. Over here."

Other Day turned toward the man and slowly dismounted.

"What happened?" Avery asked.

"Yes, tell us," Mary Ann said, coming up behind him.

Other Day nodded and smiled grimly. "I'll tell you while somebody fixes up my shoulder."

Between Avery and Mary Ann, the wound was cleaned and a bandage applied. By the time they finished, Other Day had completed his report.

"Is the Army on its way to Twin Springs?" he asked.

"Yep," Avery said. "We wired them and asked that they tell us what they were goin' to do. We got their answer about an hour later." Avery picked up the basin of bloody water and went to the door of the depot, where they had set up a sort of headquarters. No one in town except Avery, Mary Ann, and the telegraph operator had known about the drama that was unfolding.

"What are you going to do now, Other Day?" Mary Ann asked. "I hope you'll consider staying on at the Double J—no, make that the *Rocking H.* It's time to get rid of everything that was Josiah Jarting's."

"Under the circumstances, Miss Mary Ann, I think it might be wise if I got on my horse and just rode the hell out of here."

"Why, for heaven's sake?"

"Well, for one thing there're four dead white men and one dead Ute at Twin Springs. The Army'll have a lot of questions they'll want answered. They'll be showing up here in Flea Hill mighty quick, and I don't want to be anywhere around when they do."

"You've done nothing wrong, Other Day," she said. "In fact, I'd say you probably saved a lot of lives by doing what you've done."

"That's what you say. The Army might have an entirely different outlook. If they'd been notified and gone there without me interfering, Jarting and the others might very well be alive right now."

"You're just being stubborn," she said and stepped back when he stood. He walked to the door of the depot and went outside.

Mary Ann followed and they were met by Avery at the door.

"Here, Other Day," he said handing him his Stetson. "I found this in the calaboose. Is it yours?"

Other Day nodded and took the hat. He walked over to the bay and pulled the latigos tight before swinging into the saddle.

"Since John Henry Lutehoser is dead, Other Day, I'll need a foreman." She smiled at him, promising more than just the job of ramrod.

"No, thank you just the same."

"I'll need help managing the business end of the ranch, too. Please? Please, Other Day? Take the job." She stared up at him, her face serious.

"Sounds good to me," Avery said.

"It's a nice offer, Miss Mary Ann," Other Day said. "But I'll be truthful with you. I'm not all that fond of ranch life." The 'breed studied her for a long minute. Mary Ann Hyburger was a beautiful woman, tall, lithe, graceful. She owned a good ranch and she wanted him to stay. She wasn't the least bit shy when she looked at him, and the expression in her eyes promised so much more than the job she had offered.

Logan sighed heavily. The thought of Belle Doolin and her grandfather surfaced alongside the memory of Theron Cullen. He had been close to all of them and they were all dead because of him. Logan shook his head. He knew he hadn't caused the death of his friends. But it sure seemed that anyone who took on the role of friend to Other Day Logan wound up suffering in some way. If that were true, and he firmly believed it was, he would not be doing Mary Ann Hyburger or Avery Longcamp any favors if he did hang around.

He smiled grimly. "It's a nice offer, ma'am, but I can't take it. Why not consider Avery there for your foreman? I think he could probably demand the respect of your other hands—considering he's the best fighter on the ranch now."

Mary Ann nodded reluctantly and Avery shook his head. He held up his hand and Other Day took it. They shook and the 'breed nodded to him.

He touched the brim of his Stetson in salute to Mary Ann Hyburger and turned the bay. The animal leaped forward when Other Day prodded him in the sides with his boots.

"Adios!" he called over his shoulder and waved with his good arm.

Mary Ann and Avery stood near the depot, watching the half-breed ride away toward the south.

BREED

Scorned and despised by red and white men alike, half-breed Other Day Logan rode a solitary trail of vengeance. Quick to anger, slow to forgive, he lived in a twilight world where questions meant trouble and answers were found at the end of a gun.

BREED by Ned Stone. Logan's quest for revenge led him to Bell's Town, where one of the men who had raped and killed his mother had decided to hide out for a spell. But what should have been as easy as slaughtering a pig turned into a bloodbath.

__2874-3 $2.95

BREED #2: MOUNTAIN MASSACRE by Ned Stone. Upon returning to his sweetheart's home, Logan found her and her grandfather brutally murdered. He swore to avenge their deaths — no matter how many men he had to kill to do so.

__2897-2 $2.95

LEISURE BOOKS
ATTN: Customer Service Dept.
276 5th Avenue, New York, NY 10001

Please add $1.25 for shipping and handling of the first book and $.30 for each book thereafter. All orders shipped within 6 weeks via postal service book rate.

Canadian orders must reflect Canadian price, when indicated, and must be paid in U.S. dollars through a U.S. banking facility.

Name ____

Address ____

City ___________________________ State ________ Zip ______

I have enclosed $ ____________ in payment for the books checked above.